Our
Children
Are
Dying

ALSO BY NAT HENTOFF

NAT HENTOFF

Our Children
Are Dying

Introduction by JOHN HOLT

THE VIKING PRESS · NEW YORK

VIKING COMPASS EDITION
Issued in 1967 by The Viking Press, Inc.
625 Madison Avenue, New York, N.Y. 10022

Distributed in Canada by
The Macmillan Company of Canada Limited

SBN 670-53071-9 (hardbound)

SBN 670-00210-0 (paperbound)

Library of Congress catalog card number: 66-23825
Eighth printing January 1970
Printed in U.S.A.

Our Children Are Dying, in somewhat different and briefer form, first appeared in *The New Yorker* as *The Principal.* The author is grateful to *The New Yorker* for permission to use the material here.

For WILLIAM SHAWN

INTRODUCTION

Not long ago I met Elliott Shapiro for the first time. From what I had read of him, I knew I would respect and like him. Yet the man himself surprised me. He is an old-fashioned radical, of a kind that fortunately seems to be coming back into fashion. The kind of things that a lot of our best young people are trying to do, he has been doing for a long time. Like them, he is above all concerned with human beings and the way they live their lives, here and now. But he knows what many of them have yet to learn, that the way to make a society what ours in many ways is not, humane and decent, is not to try to forge instruments of power with which to take that society apart and put it together differently. The way to make a society better is to find work that needs doing and that you enjoy doing, and to do that work as well as you possibly can. He knows, in short, that you do not get real power, effective power—any more than happiness—by summoning it, or pursuing. You get it, if you get it at all, as an accidental and unlooked-for by-product of doing, right now, something that badly needs to be done.

Gentle as he is, Dr. Shapiro is a tough-minded realist. He has been bucking the system—organized power and authority—for a long time. He knows how ponderous, devious, and touchy it is. Experience has taught him that most of the time the holders and wielders of power are not to be believed, trusted, or relied on. Yet his long battle against the way things are has left him neither resigned nor embittered. In every word, look, and gesture he shows a hopefulness and enthusiasm, a conviction that every day really is a brand-new day, in which almost anything might happen, that we ordinarily find only in the best of children. He is indeed a Happy Warrior.

This book, about him and his school, raises and answers some important questions. Of these, none is more important than the question of educational leadership. What is the job of an educational leader? What is a principal or a super-intendent for? We are torn between two views. One, which generally prevails in practice, might be called the corporate or military view. The job of an educational administrator is to tell everyone under him what to do, and make sure they do it. Bill Hull told me once of visiting a superintendent of a large school system who at one point pulled his watch from his pocket, laid it firmly on the table, and said with evident pride and satisfaction, "I can tell you what every teacher in this system is doing right now." The other view, a rather violent reaction to the first, is that by and large educational administrators should be no more than busi-ness managers and should have nothing to do with educa-tion whatever. Their job is simply to keep the school build-ing equipped, heated, lighted, and clean, and to stay out of the teachers' way.

Because I am a teacher, and something of an anarchist, I lean toward the latter view. If we have to choose between authoritarian leadership in education and no leadership at all, better none at all. But the example of Dr. Shapiro shows us that the head of a school, or a system of schools, need not choose between being an absolute boss or only a sweeper of floors and payer of bills. What the good teacher can do for children, the good administrator can do for his teachers—create and maintain an environment in the highest degree favorable to their learning and growth. In a part of the city from which most teachers flee as soon as they can, Dr. Shapiro has stabilized his teaching staff ". . . by making P.S. 119 a school in which teachers felt free to experiment and in which they could depend on further support from an actively interested parent body." In short, he has seen that his duty to his teachers is neither to boss nor to ignore, but to inspire, reassure, and protect.

The book also helps to refute some currently fashionable ideas about the education of slum children. The conventional wisdom of our day has it that the reason that slum children do badly in school lies in the children. It goes on to say that the children's lack of ability and skill is not their fault, but the fault of their environment, their neighborhoods, above all their homes and families. It suggests that the trouble can be remedied by giving these children an intensive preschool training, so that they can begin school with the same skills as children in the suburbs. But, as this book shows, the diagnosis is false, and the remedy is almost certain to prove ineffective. The most important reasons for the failure of slum children's education lie not in the children but in the schools.

We are led to believe, by much of what we read, that the average slum child arrives at school something of a cross between an ignorant savage and a maniac. This is flatly untrue. Dr. Shapiro writes: "I had expected that children, growing up crowded together in broken homes, would present problems similar to those manifested by neurotic children. I have discovered that, on the whole, they do not. Most of the children here are as 'normal' as children in middle-class neighborhoods." Not long ago a friend of mine, Mrs. Lore Rasmussen, put the matter even more strongly. After many years of teaching in a suburban private school, she is now teaching first-graders in public schools in some of the poorest, most crime-infested slums of one of our large cities.

She told me that the children she now teaches are, if anything, more open, more kindly, more generous, more spontaneous, and more fun to teach and work with than the children she used to teach in private school.

If the tests that the public schools live by and swear by mean anything, there is considerable reason to believe that slum children are as much harmed by their schools as by anything else in their environment. It has been shown more than once that the differences in skill and learning between slum children and middle-class children grow greater through the school years. The slum children are not very far behind when they first come to school, but the longer they stay, the further behind they get. Even their I.Q. scores go down every year. George Dennison tells us, in *Liberation,* of a Puerto Rican boy he knows who came to this country at the age of seven, able to read Spanish, and who at the age of twelve, after five years of schooling, *was able to read neither English nor Spanish.* I suspect that his case is by no means unique.

The problem, then, is how to fix up, not the children, but the schools. Dr. Shapiro shows us much of what must be done, and could be done right now; he also suggests many other things we could do with a little more money, effort, and leadership. There is only one of his assumptions and proposals that I would like to question. It is that our problems are caused above all else by too large classes, and that the most important and perhaps essential step toward improving slum education is to reduce class size. I am not at all convinced that this is true, and in any case it seems to me almost a counsel of despair. There does not seem to me as much as a chance in a thousand that our large cities will in the near future increase their education budgets enough to make possible much reduction in class size. If anything, classes are likely to get bigger rather than smaller. For this reason, and for many others just as important, I think we must try to find ways to free children from their dependence on the teacher, and to free the teacher from the crushing burden of feeling that everything that the children learn in class they must learn *from him.* In short, we must, as I think we can, find ways to make the schools and classrooms places where children do a large part of their learning independently, without direction or supervision, or any more adult help or intervention than they ask for. To put it a bit differently, I doubt very much whether there is anywhere a slum school that, given $5000 to spend, would not do better to spend it on books and learning materials than on the salary of another teacher.

But this is a small matter, at most a very minor difference of opinion. In putting it forward, I do not mean to cast the least doubt on the excellence and importance of this portrait in action of a great educator and human being.

JOHN HOLT

Boston, Massachusetts

Indeed if any additional evidence were wanting in favour of the Superiour and commanding Excellence of this system of instruction it is to be found in this Institution the African Free School where the poor children of Colour of our City are rescued from the complicated Evils that belong to their Situation & placed in a course of mental and religious improvement that enables them to look forward to the time when . . . in part the degradation that belongs to their Colour and their shame shall be wiped off & Ethiopia shall Stretch forth her hands unshackled by Slavery and unstained by the pollutions of Ignorance and Idolatry.

— Resolution of the Common Council of the City of New York, 10 May 1824

The New York City public schools surpass in quality and in their forward momentum those of any other city in America.

— Lloyd K. Garrison, President of the New York City Board of Education, 6 May 1966

"The poor children of Colour" in New York City and elsewhere in the country are still seen by too many of their teachers and principals as "degraded" by both color and class, so "degraded" that they cannot be "motivated" to learn as much as middle-class children can.

The proof, in the public schools of New York City and other large cities, has been distilled by Dr. Kenneth Clark in a paper presented to the education group at the Planning

Session of the White House Conference "To Fulfill These Rights," November 16–18, 1965.

Schools segregated by class and color, Clark emphasized, are characterized by:

1. marked cumulative academic retardation in a disproportionately high percentage of the children who attend these schools; the process begins in the third or fourth grade and increases through the eighth grade;
2. a high percentage of dropouts in the junior and senior high schools; these students are characteristically unequipped academically and occupationally for a constructive role in society;
3. a pattern of rejection and despair and hopelessness resulting in massive human wastage.

This is a book about some of these children, but it is not intended as simply another voyeuristic look at a slum school: See the culturally deprived children. See the violent children. See the foully swearing children. And see the poor, beleaguered teacher trying to teach. That kind of approach too often leads to the conclusion, as one educator has blandly put it, that "there is an internal perfection about poverty and deprivation which tends to regenerate its separate evils and to defeat scattered efforts. Any real hope of change requires reforms across the board, and not merely in the schools."

Are we then to tell the children now in slum schools—and their parents—to wait until the "across the board" changes are made? The thrust of this book is that we need not tell them that. And we cannot, for they know when they're being conned.

Nor, on the other hand, do I claim that Elliott Shapiro, whose lifework and life style are the substance of this book, performs educative miracles. In his school too children are dying, but fewer are dying than if he were not there. And his concepts of education, if applied in slum schools throughout the country, could save many more children—and now.

Furthermore, Elliott Shapiro's way of educating is relevant to all schools, not only schools in the ghettos. As John Holt has underlined in *How Children Fail* (Pitman): "Even in the kindest and gentlest of schools, children are afraid, many of them a great deal of the time, some of them almost all the time . . . afraid of failing, afraid of being kept back, afraid of being called stupid, afraid of feeling themselves stupid."

Fear is not unknown in Elliott Shapiro's school, but it is far less pervasive than in most other schools. And there is no fear whatsoever of the principal, because he and his concern for them are palpably real to the children. Accordingly, they respond to him not as an abstract authority figure but as the man he is. The nature of that man, in the context of public education in slum schools, is the subject of this book.

NAT HENTOFF

Our
Children
Are
Dying

I

During recent years of looking into the New York City public school system in what are euphemistically known as "disadvantaged" neighborhoods, I have listened to vehement condemnations of many schools by parents, civil rights activists, and unaffiliated but concerned adults in the community. The complaints most frequently focus on teachers who appear to be convinced that Negro and Puerto Rican students have limited capacities for learning and on principals who have insulated themselves from the children—and the neighborhood. But in visits to Central Harlem, I've noted that these indictments invariably except one elementary school and its principal—P.S. 119 and Dr. Elliott Shapiro. Mrs. Thelma Johnson, for instance, a former official of the Harlem Parents Committee, regards Shapiro as being "beyond category." In Harlem, she says, "we either get principals who consider their work as just a job, a certain number of hours to be filled, or occasionally we get a liberal. The liberal feels he must help the heathen, but since he does indeed see the children as heathen, his attitude precludes his being of any help. Elliott sees them as children, and he has a strong sense of the importance—and individuality—of each one of them." In November 1964, for another example of the community's feeling about Shapiro, a testimonial dinner was held for the principal by a neighborhood association—the Community League of West 159th Street—in conjunction with the staff of P.S. 119 and the parents of its pupils. Among the tributes to Dr. Shapiro was an appraisal by Ralph Edwards, a slight, taut Negro teacher at the school: "His concerns are not empathic in the clinical sense which treats each separate instance of suffering with the same 'detached' sympathy, emphasizing interest rather than involvement. No, Elliott Shapiro learned a long time ago that we are all in trouble, himself included. He finds it impossible to be detached from a condition in which he is so inextricably involved."

Curious, in the spring of 1965 I began a series of visits to the school and the involved principal. The most immediate mark of the neighborhood's poverty is its idle men. In midmorning, men stand, like statues, in front of storefronts on Eighth Avenue and on the stoops of decayed brownstones along 133rd Street, where the school is located, off Eighth Avenue. Most of the men stand alone. P.S. 119, built in 1899, is bleak and forbidding. A massive five-story structure, with its cornices and towers it is medieval in appearance. Whatever their original color may have been, its bricks have weathered into a sickly beige. The only relief from the gloom are bright patches of color from children's drawings in the windows. When I started my visits, next to P.S. 119, its replacement was under construction, and in February 1966, P.S. 119 yielded to P.S. 92.

On the ground floor of P.S. 119, a sign pointed to the prin-

cipal's office on the floor above. At the head of the stair-
case, on the wall to the right, were pictures in color of Nigerian political leaders; circus cutouts in orange construction
paper; and a display, titled WHAT WOULD YOU LIKE TO BE?, with
pictures and descriptions of various professions (Organic
Chemist, Histologist, Satellite Tracker, Medical Social Worker,
Radar System Designer). On the opposite wall were pictures
of Phillis Wheatley, Booker T. Washington, Martin Luther
King, Sidney Poitier, and Constance Baker Motley. Beneath
each was an essay on the luminary by one of the students.
Next to that exhibit a poster announced a BOOK FAIR FOR
CHILDREN AND ADULTS sponsored by the Parents' Association
of P.S. 119.

The office, I note, is distinctly different from principals' offices in most other elementary schools I've visited. Instead
of the customary unsmiling, impersonal attitude of the secretaries, the office personnel seem to erect no barriers of not-to-
be-questioned authority between themselves and the children who come in and out bearing messages or wanting to
see the principal. Busy but relaxed, the secretaries talk to,
rather than at, the children. At the back of the room, on the
left, is Dr. Shapiro's small private office. Its door is almost
always open. In his mid-fifties, six feet tall but slightly
stooped, gray-haired, Shapiro has the face of a watchful
but gentle eagle. He is soft-spoken and often wry. "It's like
a medieval castle, isn't it?" He points to the battlements outside his window. "When it rains and the yard gets flooded,
all you need is a drawbridge."

As Shapiro began to walk out of his office into the outer
room, a wiry eight-year-old girl in a white sweater and flowered skirt walked by the secretaries and stopped him. He
leaned down to listen. "Dr. Shapiro, do you know where they
put the books you can buy from the book fair? I wrote down
the one I want." He took a slip of paper from her and read

it. "You're a little bit late, Debbie, but I'll try to save one for you. I think we have some of those left." "I don't have any money, but I'll have it later." Shapiro nodded and she waved good-by. "Thank you for coming," he said.

There are eleven hundred children in the school in classes from pre-kindergarten through the sixth grade. The area served is from 129th Street north to 134th Street and from St. Nicholas Avenue east to Seventh Avenue. It is what social workers call a high delinquency neighborhood. About thirty-five per cent of its families are on welfare and the rest have low-income jobs. "The level of family income," Shapiro says, "is from forty to seventy dollars a week. Almost all the parents earn so little that their children qualify for free lunch." (Later I discovered that some of the parents too come in for free lunch.)

"As for housing," Shapiro continued, "our *middle*-income housing is the low-income St. Nicholas housing project. They send us about three hundred and fifty children. The housing conditions for many others are very bad. Across the street a house built for eight families has forty-five. Next door there are two houses with serious heating problems. Two winters ago, I spent hours trying to track down the owner, and finally I told the man who said he was only the agent that if heat weren't provided, there'd be a picket line of teachers and me. There was heat for the rest of the winter. The next year there was no heat again and we couldn't even find the agent. Finally the city took it over as a public nuisance. Another time for another building, we found someone in the Mayor's office who was vulnerable to picketing and he arranged for the city to take that one over. Nonetheless, the furnace remained broken, and it took us fifteen days of constant pressure to get it fixed. People talk about the 'apathy' of the people here. Well, all of us middle-class 'respectable' forces, including a neighborhood priest, couldn't

get any action for *fifteen days* in the dead of winter with
people sick in the building. How do you expect poor people to
have confidence *they* can get anything done?"

I mentioned my surprise that a principal would get himself involved in neighborhood housing problems. "Our
school," Shapiro answered, "has to have an organic relationship with the community. If the staff tries to take action, that
indicates to the community that there *is* hope. *Then* the parents come alive; and in any case, what happens in the street
affects our children. Education that stops at three in the afternoon is mis-education."

About ninety-six per cent of the children, Shapiro continued, are Negro. The rest are Puerto Rican, along with a
few Chinese children. "We haven't had a white child since
1958." The average class size is 28.3, a little lower than the
city average for elementary schools, which is 30.5. "But
it's still far too large for our purposes," Shapiro emphasized.
"There should be one adult to twelve children, and never
more than one to twenty-two. For certain children, one
adult for three is right. For some, one for one. And I can
think of cases where two adults for one child is the proper
ratio."

The little girl in the flowered skirt was back. She gave
Shapiro an envelope. "The money's in there." He took it.
"When you leave money with someone, Debbie, you should
ask for a receipt." "Uh-huh." Shapiro made out a receipt and
gave it to her. She put it in her pocket, giggled, and walked
away. "Don't lose it," Shapiro said after her.

I observed that the child hadn't been at all constrained
about interrupting while Shapiro was talking with an adult.
"Oh," he said, "we encourage interruptions. Many of our
children are not in real communication with adults. So we
have to bring adults into their lives, adults they can depend on
and feel at ease with. Coming from large families, often with

working mothers and no fathers, our children lose their child-hood too early. They become self-reliant, in one sense, too soon. When they're seven or eight, they're as self-reliant as a middle-class young adult. But a dependency relationship with an adult is necessary for children. They should have a long childhood because there's so much to learn. And the school has to be the place where they can be children—a specially created world in which small events are important and in which they can discuss those events with an adult they trust. That's why I keep coming back to the need for smaller classes.

"These interruptions," he continued, "often consist of complaints. The fact that the children have someone—an adult —who listens means that they don't have to be quite so self-reliant, they don't have to take the law into their hands. It means that they can remain children."

We walked into the hall and a gaggle of children rushed by. "They look lively, don't they?" said Shapiro. "And they're very charming. But our children are dying. The way they look conceals the fact that they're dying. It's not like being killed by a car. There's no blood on them, and because there is no visible injury, nobody in the middle class is aghast at the sight. Nobody gets really involved. Let me give you an example of what I mean. Fourteen years ago, two years before I came here, of one hundred and twenty-two children in the sixth grade, only three were reading at grade level. That means one hundred and nineteen children had been separated very effectively from society. They're now twenty-five or twenty-six years old. What kinds of jobs do you think they have? I don't know for sure, but I can make an informed guess. That year one hundred and nineteen children died. And thousands and thousands of other children in this city have been dying because their brain cells have never been fully brought to life. But the white middle class doesn't *see* this. Living in a ghetto, the children are out of sight and out of conscience."

A twelve-year-old boy ambled along the corridor. "Hi," Shapiro waved. The boy smiled. Miss Carmen I. Jones, a Negro, an assistant principal in charge of the lower grades from pre-kindergarten through the second grade, joined us as we walked. "We did begin to do a little better," Shapiro went on, "but not nearly well enough. By 1961, of one hundred and sixty-seven children in the sixth grade, forty-five were reading at grade level or above. That doesn't mean the children fourteen years ago were inferior. It means that we were helping some of our children learn to read somewhat more effectively. But since, in this affluent economy, education is still financed out of a principle of scarcity, there was a precipitous drop in the achievement level of that 1961 sixth grade below the top forty-five. We were too badly outnumbered to give the rest of those sixth graders all they needed. And they died. One example of how outnumbered we were is that from 1955 to 1962 the first and second grades and part of the third grade were on double shifts. They'd come in from eight to twelve or from twelve to four. They didn't even get a full day of schooling. Now that's stopped, but we're still outnumbered.

"From 1961 on, in terms of sixth-grade reading levels, we've been going downhill. The reason is that, after the third grade, we send our best achievers away to Intellectually Gifted Children's classes. We encourage parents to use the free-choice transfer policy to send their children to schools with an I.G.C. Program in other areas, thereby also promoting integrated education. Sure, losing their very best achievers is discouraging for our teachers, but we owe it to the children to let them get into those I.G.C. classes. When we move into our new school, I'm going to try to develop our own I.G.C. Program and then encourage class leaders from other schools to come to us. Better yet, obviously, would be heterogeneous classes with children at varying achievement levels. But to make those work, you need much, much smaller ratios of adults to children."

I asked whether the I.G.C. classes weren't harmful in the sense that they might create a feeling among those selected of being part of an elite, and a feeling of inferiority among those left out.

"As long," said Miss Jones firmly, "as they have those programs in other neighborhoods and other schools, we have to follow the concept."

"Besides," Shapiro added, "it doesn't hurt for a Negro child to feel superior."

"But," Miss Jones countered sharply, "they feel superior to other Negro children."

"That's why," Shapiro said, "I try to have our bright achievers sent into other neighborhoods than predominantly Negro ones."

I asked about the current emphasis on preschool training, such as the Head Start program that has been sponsored by the Federal government. "It's important," Shapiro began, "but it's hardly the whole answer. The lives of our children get worse as they grow older, primarily because the lives of their parents get worse. As our children age, when something unusual happens, it's usually something bad. And simultaneously their responsibilities increase. They have more younger siblings to take care of, and their mothers are forced to become more distant as *their* problems and number of children increase. That's why we have to build more and more of an inner protection against the worsening of their lives as they become older. In the kindergarten and the first grade, for instance, there are more children of unbroken families than in the fifth or sixth grades. It gets harder and harder for the fathers to find employment that will bring in enough money and that will also keep their egos intact. And as fathers, precisely because they have self-respect, can no longer fulfill their ego ideals, they begin to disappear. I remember that during the Depression we didn't know what to do with ourselves. But the Negro male in a neighborhood like this is in a permanent Depression much worse than that of the 1930s.

"Therefore, a Project Head Start by itself is not enough. The whole system has to be radically improved. Moreover, the emphasis on the need for preschool educational experience often leads to the assumption that nearly all our children begin school badly damaged. Well, four years ago, we decided to compare a group of children from three schools in poor neighborhoods—one of them P.S. 119—and three schools from middle-class sections. We tested kindergarten children and first-graders who had not gone to kindergarten; and we tested them in their first weeks in class, before they had become contaminated by schooling. We expected great disparity between the Harlem children and the others. Actually, while twenty-five per cent of our children were severely deprived, the other seventy-five per cent were much closer to middle-class norms in terms of knowledge and in terms of their apperceptive abilities than most people had given them credit for. It is *after* the first grade that the disparities between our children and those of the middle class start showing up."

Shapiro had to return to his office for an appointment, and I went into the teachers' room on the second floor, where Carmen Jones introduced me to Mrs. Jean Boone, who teaches reading in the fifth and sixth grades. She was having lunch with Albert Marcus, a fifth-grade teacher. I asked them how they would characterize Dr. Shapiro's style as a principal.

Slim, intense, Mrs. Boone thought for a few moments.

"There's never anything overwhelming about it," she said. "Only gradually do you realize there is leadership, but it's not in the conventional administrative sense. He's neither a machine like many other principals nor is he so chaotically involved that he runs around like a teacher trainee, as some others do. How can I make it tangible? He's a constant stimulus. Here we're all free to initiate ideas and practices. And if they don't work out, you're not made to feel stupid. I don't think anyone on the staff feels hampered. That's why the turnover of teachers is low and why many volunteer to teach here. Another thing is that he *listens*."

"Unlike," Marcus broke in, "those principals who don't want to be bothered with problems. In those schools, if you have a child in trouble, it's like *your* fault. It has nothing to do with *them*."

"It's a funny way he listens, though," said Mrs. Boone. "Often, all of a sudden, you find yourself answering your own questions and finding your own answers."

A teacher walked over with a can for contributions.

"Red Cross?" asked Marcus.

"Tomorrow," she said. "Today I'm collecting cancer."

"There's no pressure here," Mrs. Boone was still trying to be precise about Shapiro's style.

"And that lack of pressure," Marcus added, "reaches the kids. You can be yourself and you can let them be themselves—if that's the way you teach. Many of these kids, after they finish the sixth grade, keep coming back. You almost have to chase them on to their new school."

"They feel accepted here," Mrs. Boone said. "They get a sense of their own presence. And they feel as free to go to Shapiro as they do to their teacher. Sometimes freer. I've heard *little* children say to a teacher, 'I'm going to tell Dr. Shapiro on you.' And they don't have to go far to find him. He wanders a lot. He knows what's going on. It's the oddest thing. If there's a crisis anywhere in the school, he's *there.*"

"You know what it is?" said Marcus. "The school is alive. You go into some elementary schools and everything is quiet, much too quiet. But these kids are suppressed in small, over-crowded apartments. They need a place to express them-selves. And this is the place. But he can't perform miracles. We need more money for books and for materials. Like when we're working in Negro history, there aren't enough books to cover more than one class at a time."

"And we need smaller classes!" Mrs. Boone almost shouted.

"Every child over twenty in a class is one too many," said Marcus.

"Every child over fifteen," Mrs. Boone corrected him. "I've taken children on my own in groups of three and four, and they've gotten so much out of it. It's worked even with absolute nonreaders. *Then* I got results. Also we need more money to help build a range of experiences for the children. I don't mean Higher Horizons where you take a group of kids somewhere for 'cultural enrichment,' and they all meet outside the school, still segregated. I mean the kinds of ex-periences in which they're integrated with children of back-grounds that are varied economically and socially as well as racially. All sorts of children ought to take trips together, and our kids ought to be able to participate in other schools' activities—like sharing a science fair. And children from other schools ought to come here and work in our science fair."

"It would also be valuable," Marcus said, "for some of the teachers in other schools to get to know our kids. Those stereotypes about children of the poor are still so pervasive. 'They can't learn.' 'They won't learn.' It's surprising how much they do learn with all the obstacles against them. Last year I had thirty-three in my class."

"Oh, they have strengths," Mrs. Boone said mordantly. "The ability to survive, for one. And look at the amount of responsibility these children have to take. Little children picking up littler children and bringing them home. They can't enjoy growing up because they can't be children."

"They get away with being children here," Marcus broke in. "I've seen Shapiro tell a child that if he's hurt, he should cry. He'll soothe them and make them feel important. To an adult their problems often seem so little, but he sees those problems as the child does. Yesterday a kid came into his office because he'd lost his coat, and Shapiro scurried around looking for another coat for him until he could find his own."

"In some of my classes when I first came here," said Mrs. Boone, "it took a great deal of effort to make the children realize you *wanted* to talk to them. And when the realization came, they were overwhelmed. They all began to talk at once. It was a paradox, but I had to be a disciplinarian to allow for informality. I had to set up a structure within which they could have freedom to express themselves. They had to learn that their opinions were acceptable, and before that, some of them had to learn they *had* opinions. You see, one thing they do learn in order to survive is how to build defenses against danger. They go inside themselves. But in constructing those defenses, some ward off learning too—unless you can get to them. And I don't always get to them." She lit a cigarette. "There are days when I don't feel I'm accomplishing *anything*. The children have been frustrated so long, I feel like I'm sitting on a powder keg."

Marcus nodded in agreement. "But they do sense," he said, "when someone's in their corner."

"Yes." Mrs. Boone leaned forward. "We Negroes are on guard against so many things because we're put on the defensive all our lives. And so, Negro teachers can sense a phony too. I worked in a school with a principal who was afraid of the kids. He was afraid to *touch* them. Shapiro pulls them in. Before you know it, there's a child in his arms." She smiled. "I walked in last week and he was comforting a boy who had ripped his pants while at the same time he was trying to sew the tear. I had to take the needle away from him. Sewing is not one of his major skills. And the community senses his realness too. I was with him one day when a stranger stopped him on Eighth Avenue. 'You ain't just the principal of the school,' the man said. 'You're the principal of this neighborhood.' That testimonial dinner a couple of years ago didn't begin at P.S. 119. It started outside. People in the neighborhood felt the guy should be honored and they came to us just for last-minute help. He was certainly embarrassed by all that praise."

Mrs. Boone was silent for a few seconds. "You know, I never think of him in terms of color. With some people, I always have in the back of my mind, 'What does this white guy want?' But I've stopped thinking of him as a white man. He's almost become a 'member.'"

A young Negro teacher, listening in, laughed. "I don't think of him as a 'member,'" she said. "I know he's a Jewish man with a long, hooked nose. But I know he cares about these kids, and that's what counts."

"Sometimes," Marcus said abstractedly, "I have a fantasy —Shapiro as Superintendent of Schools."

"Huh!" Mrs. Boone pushed back her coffee cup and rose. "If they ever made him Superintendent, they'd also revise the city charter so that he'd just be a figurehead. Or if they did give him power, he'd have a hell of a lot of resistance from many of the principals and the other supervisory personnel. They don't want to move in any new directions. They just want to make it, day by day. They wouldn't know how to handle the freedom he'd give them, and they'd take their anxieties out on him."

II

A few mornings later, I was at P.S. 119 a little after nine for an assembly on the fourth floor. As I walked in, I noticed Shapiro standing at the back of the auditorium. At the front, a buxom woman, Mrs. Bonnie Taylor, announced that the assembly was being dedicated to Dr. Shapiro. He winced. Eleven girls stood and sang in unison:

"Oh he is the bravest
Oh he is the greatest
We'll fight before we switch!"

"Talk about brainwashing," Shapiro mumbled, slumped in a back row seat. The children performed—some singing, others reciting. From time to time Shapiro looked around the room. At one point he said softly, "You see that plumpish girl with the brown blouse in the center of the back row? We may lose her, I'm afraid. Her mother is known in the area as a quasi-prostitute, and the other kids used to tease her unmercifully. She'd react with various kinds of aggression and was very difficult to handle. Then I put her in Mrs. Taylor's class. It's an unusual class in that it includes children from the second to the sixth grades who need extra support—who need to be able to believe that an adult cares enough about them to protect them. When they're strong enough, they leave her room to go into their regular grade classes. Mrs. Taylor has forbidden the children in her room to tease that girl, but the child has other problems too. I don't know how long we'll be able to hold her.

"I started that class," Shapiro continued in a whisper, "in 1954. So far as I know, only a few principals in other schools have since tried similar projects. For eight years, we also had a second-grade class for children who had been severely rejected by their parents or whose home situation was especially catastrophic in other ways. These were kids who had to be softened up by close contact, often physical contact."

"You mean," I said, "mothering them? Holding them?" I added that I asked because, in passing a classroom that morning, I had seen a young teacher, whom I later found out to be Lawrence Greenfield, with his arms around a boy. The boy's face was on Greenfield's chest, and Greenfield was patting him gently on the back.

"Yes," Shapiro answered. "In fact, Greenfield had that second-grade class for a couple of years. But I found that teachers couldn't take the strain for more than a year or two, and two years ago I discontinued it because I didn't have a teacher for it at the time. But Mrs. Taylor seems indestructible. She has the kind of bull strength of a King Canute ordering the waves to go back. The most aggressive children soon learn they can't act out against her, and they also learn that she'll protect them against the aggression of others. She visits the homes and makes the relatively few mothers who reject their children toe the line too and support the children.

Usually she starts out with a class of about ten, but it increases as the year goes on. Right now she has forty. In addition she comes in very early to be in charge of the yard and she works in the after-school center."

Mrs. Taylor asked Dr. Shapiro to say a few words. He rose, his stoop more pronounced than usual, went to the front of the room, looked at the children, and said, "I'm very moved by this unexpected treat. I've had very few assembly programs dedicated to me, and I think it's more than I deserve. Thank you very much." He returned to his back-row seat. "Oh, well," he smiled, "I didn't realize until just now that today is April Fool's Day."

A thin, alert girl with pigtails and blue-tinted glasses began to conduct an instrumental ensemble. "That's Doreen. She looks charming, doesn't she?" said Shapiro. "She has very severe problems of aggression. She's in Mrs. Taylor's class too."

I wondered how Shapiro was able to know so many of the children by name and condition. "I'm not doing as well as I used to," he answered. "A school isn't worth much unless the principal knows every child by name, but I'm falling behind."

A teacher walked by and Shapiro identified him as Richard Stephenson, a fifth-grade teacher. A brisk man in his early thirties, Stephenson had found out about P.S. 119 a couple of years before, while engaged in a remedial reading project for Negro children in Prince Edward County, Virginia. He had come to see Shapiro and had been hired.

"He's a very resourceful teacher," Shapiro observed. "He uses all kinds of teaching methods. Montessori, role playing—anything that seems to work. When he started with his present class, they were below the national average in reading, but they've been moving up. He's had them putting together a computer, for example. That stimulated them to read better because they wouldn't have been able to assemble it without understanding the instructions. He also makes considerable use of volunteer helpers among the mothers. That project started with his belief mothers should visit the class whenever they felt like it. More and more did, and some stayed to help. He visits the homes, sends messages, and is quick to give publicity to the parents who encourage the children to do their homework conscientiously. He cites them in a class paper the children put out. The way the children got the computer kit was by selling cookies. From the proceeds of that they bought stock in a bowling ball company. When the stock went up, they sold it and bought the kit."

A lean boy of about twelve, wearing a green jacket, old black pants, and a pork-pie hat, walked up the aisle. His head was down. "Hello, John," said Shapiro. The boy didn't look up and kept going.

"There's a remarkable boy." Shapiro looked after him. "He's in the sixth grade and reads at an eleventh-grade level. I don't really understand how it happened. He doesn't know who his mother was. He does know he has a father somewhere who has no interest in him. Some years ago, he was picked up by a woman who became his mother. She was an alcoholic and a quasi-prostitute, but she gave the child real warmth. Sometimes we'd see them hanging on to each other, almost crying on each other. A few months ago the man with whom she had been living died. And soon after, she died. The man had been brutal and used to whip the boy, but with the woman there, there was at least someone in the house on whom he could depend. Now he and his younger sister are being taken care of by another woman. He calls her an 'aunt.' She doesn't care much for John, and the man she's living with has no use for him. There have been weekends during which he's had no food, and we've tried to intervene. When there's no food in the house, his younger sister, Denice, has eaten with neighbors, but John says he refuses to beg for food. When it gets too bad, he goes out and hustles and then buys what he wants. He's disgusted with the kind of life his 'aunt' and 'uncle' live, but he's not sure he can get out of it."

Shapiro was beckoned by a teacher and he walked to the door. I saw a teacher I knew and asked her for more information about John. "I sure remember that 'mother' of his," she said, smiling. "She'd come in reeking, high as a kite. But in her crazy, drunk way she loved the boy. She was a harmless drunk. She made some money from numbers, but there were times I couldn't figure out how they survived. But she was a fighter. He has signs of some kind of heart strain, and she'd have to take him down to Bellevue for pills. Well, if they made her wait too long, sometimes she'd raise such a ruckus the police had to be called. They'd telephone the school and we'd calm them down.

"That's one thing about ghetto communities. One way or another, people who have nowhere to go get taken care of. Last week a little girl in my class was looking out the window as the fire engines came screaming up. I rushed to see the fire, which was across the street. The girl said matter-of-factly, 'That's my house that's burning.' It was like she'd had so much happen to her that it was hard to get excited about just a fire. Anyway, by late afternoon, she, her three brothers, and her parents had places to stay. And all in this same block. But, as for John, if he had been in any other school but this one, he would have fallen apart completely."

Shapiro had returned. "John," he said, "has always been difficult, but in recent months, he's become worse. He gets angry at the slightest provocation—or with no provocation at all. A few weeks ago, he was walking through a gym where a small class of mentally retarded children were playing. John took the basketball from one of them, the child complained, and John kicked him in the stomach. Stephenson was called, dragged him down to the office, and insisted John shouldn't be in the school. He wanted to bring charges against him in the police station but I said that wasn't our style in this school. We take calculated risks, and the kind of pressure Stephenson wanted to apply through the police would have limited our chances to experiment. Well, the next day three policemen from the Youth Squad showed up. Stephenson *had* lodged a complaint. I'm not saying he might not have had a grievance. John *seemed* dangerous, and it could have been claimed that he was in the way of educating the other children. But here grievances are taken up with the school's staff relations committee or with the union's grievances committee. Or he could have appealed above me in the system. But the police just didn't seem to be the proper agency. There's no question that Stephenson is an unusually creative teacher, but he has a tendency to overprotect his children, probably because he's aware that our children certainly do need more protection than they receive." Shapiro sighed. "I'm going to have to count up to fifty million before I talk to him about this business with the police. I do very much respect his defending his children, but I wish he'd had more trust in our attempts to help John."

The assembly over, we walked out into the corridor. "This morning," Shapiro said, "John complained for the first time—in advance of retribution by him—of being hit by somebody. We must take advantage of that. George, a boy in the sixth grade, has been picking on him for two days, and he threatened John again before school started. John can take care of George, but what's significant is that he feels ready to ask for help. Until now *everything* has been a threat to John because he felt he had nobody to speak for him. John may be the smartest boy we ever had. I've seen him come in, complaining violently, banging on a desk, but if there are books there and he sees them, he'll forget what angered him and start to read. I've never seen anything like it."

I asked what had happened with the police. "It started badly. Mrs. Olga LaBeet, one of our guidance counselors, and I began to explain how bright he was. So they asked him to read something for them. He flatly refused and told them to go away, swearing at them. That made them think Stephenson was right. But they were impressed that John is never absent, that, with no direction from home, he gets here every day. And I spoke to them at length about his potential and my anger at what Stephenson had done. That seemed to move them. Finally they made out a file card—which they lose anyway—and he was able to stay. But we did feel John could be helped by one of the caseworkers with the Bureau of Attendance. The problem was we couldn't get a caseworker unless John's problem concerned attendance in some way. Well, he does occasionally run out of a classroom, so technically, he's sometimes absent from class, and we got him a caseworker."

I saw John coming up the corridor. Behind him was a woman, whom Dr. Shapiro identified as Mrs. LaBeet. Surly, John said to Shapiro, "I bet you don't even know where George *is*." "I know, and I'm going to talk to him." John moved on. "He's always testing me," Shapiro noted. "This time he wants to see if I'll follow through now that he's complained in front, before he starts fighting. One way or another, that testing keeps going on. Right after the incident which led to Stephenson's calling the police, John started swearing at me. He and I were alone on a landing outside the gym. He called me a number of obscenities—with 'white' at the head of each list. Then he started swinging at me. I kept my hands up so I wouldn't get hurt, and looking right into his eyes, I told him, 'I'm letting you do this because I can guard against being hurt. The reason you hit little kids, like the kid with the basketball, is because those are the only kinds of problems so far you think you can take care of at the time they happen. You have very hard problems, John, and we can help you with them.' 'I don't need your help, you white bastard,' he said. Finally I told him I was going downstairs and that he could come if he wanted to. After a while, he followed me to the office, hung around, and found something to read.

"A few weeks later, he challenged me to box him. He had to reassure himself that physically I *could* take care of him. That way, if I were going to help him, my help would be worthwhile by his criteria. In other words, was I 'soft' only because I was helpless? You know, the man who lived with the 'mother' who took care of John before she died was very cruel, but John missed his beatings in a way because he felt a man as strong as that could give him some kind of security. So he came into my office, I closed the door, and we boxed for about three minutes. Mostly I outfeinted him, although occasionally I'd hit him lightly on the face. He was really trying, but he was quite pleased that he lost, because now he felt I could take care of him."

I asked how long John had been in the school.

"He started here, but we haven't had him for the full six years," said Shapiro. "While he was in the third grade, the people he was living with moved out of the district. Late in his fifth-grade year, we heard that he had gotten into considerable trouble in his new school and was about to be suspended. We were able to get him back through a waiver of district lines. For some time this year, we've been letting him do office work when he can't stay still in class. He wasn't relating to his sixth-grade teacher. At first we'd let him walk around the building. I'd know he wasn't in class when little kids would come into the office complaining that he'd bothered them. But once he began to get office work to do, he'd gravitate there. He also began to see Mrs. Lanckton, a woman who has volun-

teered to work here as counselor to the children and as con-
ductor of very small groups in reading and math with the
very young children.

"Some people on the staff," Shapiro continued, "were annoyed that John was allowed to leave his classroom when he
wanted to. They felt he was being given privileges that would
make the other children jealous. Moreover, they said, this was
not the way to educate a child. Another source of complaint
was some of the parents who work four hours a day as school
aides. They get $1.65 an hour for supervising the yards, help-
ing with lunch, assisting in the library and the stockroom,
working some of the office machines. We have fifteen aides
—more than most schools—and we have that many only because we put up a battle. But we need more. They not only
take some weight off the teachers, but they can spread messages throughout the community. When we don't have enough
books or something else needs widespread support, they can
help stir up the other parents. And we encourage that. However, in this case, some of the aides working in the office
didn't like the fact that John, without instruction, just by
watching, was doing the Thermofaxing and mimeographing
better than they were.

"John doesn't get paid officially, but I give him two dollars
every Friday. I've also taken him out to lunch a few times.
The first time, he wouldn't accept the lunch. He stood outside
the restaurant. He couldn't trust that kind of indication of
good will at that point. He didn't trust me, and he didn't
trust himself. I mean he didn't feel *he* had enough merit to
warrant his receiving anything good. The following times,
however, he did eat with me."

Mrs. LaBeet, a short woman of about forty, who seemed
to combine sizable quantities of firmness, enthusiasm, and
sensitivity, had joined the discussion. "A friend of mine said to
me"—Mrs. LaBeet was indignant—" 'Why do you let this John

cheat the other children?' He's not cheating them *that* much.
Not compared to how much the Board of Education is cheating them. I think we can be of some help to that child. But
what happens to him after he leaves here?"

Shapiro nodded. "The boy could be in one of the professions, but the odds against him are so large. He's becoming
an adolescent, and although an adolescent goes through a
period of breaking away from his parents, he also relies on
them in some ways during that process. After he leaves the
school, we could be helpful in a parental sense if he felt free
to come back, knowing we'd always be interested in what
he was doing. But what will happen to him in junior high
school with six to eight different teachers for him to cope
with? All he needs is to get into trouble with one, and then
what?"

After a glance at his watch, Shapiro returned to his office,
and I walked along with Mrs. LaBeet. "The biggest problem
with our children," she was saying, "is their uncertainty. They
have to worry about too many things. Problems are always
hanging in the air. For some, the problem is as basic as
'Where am I going to live tomorrow, and with whom?' If
there's a father in the house, is he going to walk off? Or, if
he has gone, is he ever coming back? A boy was acting up the
other day and he yelled at me, 'Go ahead and put me out
of the school! My father will take care of me!' I know who
his father is, and I know his father hasn't seen him in two
years. What he has at home is a mother with two other boys,
and all three boys are troublesome. Sure, she loves them,
but she's in a state of constant irritation. So this child fanta-
sizes about a father who'll take care of him.

"Of course,"—Mrs. LaBeet motioned to a running boy to
slow down—"many of the children are themselves in a constant state of irritation. And our means of mass communication
have sharpened their discontent. Everybody nowadays has a

TV set. These kids look at those fathers in the neat suits, they see those delicious meals and comfortable homes on the screen, and they look at where *they* are. At least before TV there were only the movies, and if you were poor, you couldn't go too often. Now the whole business is shoved down their throats every day.

"A school like this can help. But there are eighteen hours a day when they're not here. Sometimes it's the bright ones who are destroyed first. They're more acutely aware of the gap between what they see on TV and the unemployed men they see standing on the streets, to say nothing of their own lack of enough food and clothes. So you try to teach them, but on some days, it's as if they pull a shade down between themselves and you. And you can't get in there."

We walked into a sixth-grade classroom. The room was dark. On a screen at the front of the room, a series of slides describing various occupations was being shown. A resonant voice on the soundtrack talked about the different jobs and about the need for advanced education in today's world. Only a few of the children were watching. The others were whispering to each other or looking out the window.

"It's already taken root in some of them," said Mrs. LaBeet. "The so-what attitude. This is the lowest of the sixth grades."

"Where do you start?" boomed the voice on the soundtrack. "In a job where you can see a future, where you can learn and grow. If you're a dropout and go looking for a job, you have to hope the other people also looking don't have high school and college degrees."

"You look at these children and you *know* they have as much potential as middle-class children," Mrs. LaBeet said. "But they're going to get lost. How many? I say hopefully— because I have to have hope—that it's too soon to know. But in a class like this, too many."

The final slide showed a white mother, a curly-haired

child, and a resplendently furnished home—the rewards of education. "These kids," Mrs. LaBeet grimaced at the screen, "learn early to screen things out that don't seem relevant, that don't seem real to them. They feel there are too many adult voices like that one talking at them but not really concerned with what *they* want and need. How much can we do here? Some leave not yet lost. But there's so much more to be done here and throughout the city. Not only smaller classes but teachers who really know Negro and Puerto Rican culture. And many more Negroes and Puerto Ricans in positions of authority so the kids can see not only whites get to the top."

I asked Mrs. LaBeet what kept *her* trying to raise the shade. She laughed. "I do like children, and my own background at home was such that we were all taught to feel responsibility for our own people. I live in New Rochelle, and I keep busy fighting the school board there. I could have taught there too, but I decided to work in Harlem because I felt these kids especially needed Negro teachers like me. I don't want to sound egocentric, but I was brought up in a neighborhood like this and I was as poor as they are. I did have a father and mother interested in my education, but I can identify with the children. When they behave in annoying ways, I remember that, although I'm middle-class now, there were days when I acted like that. There are other Negro teachers here who were brought up in this kind of neighborhood and the kids relate better, by and large, to teachers who have been through what they know. We can see their strengths. We know they can take care of themselves better than any middle-class children in the city, and we try to broaden those strengths. In other neighborhoods, it's taken as a matter of course that a child's strengths have to be developed along many different lines. Here all those positive energies are first channeled into just surviving. But we have to do more than that. We have to give them confidence they can do more. But some first have to learn they can be loved.

"That's why what Mrs. Taylor does is so important. If you walked in at the wrong time," Mrs. LaBeet laughed, "you might not understand what's going on in her room. Like once a very big boy was threatening her. 'O.K.,' she said, 'let's go, sweetie.' And she showed him she could take care of him. But then she said, 'Come to Mother,' and kissed him while he put his head on her bosom. She doesn't reject them. She may raise Cain with them, but she doesn't reject them. She does set up restrictions, but they're within the framework of love, and they help the child begin to develop his own inner controls so that he doesn't fall off the edge.

"In her apartment, she has a room that belongs to the children. She'll take some home to dinner, some for weekends. She's taken the whole class to the show or to the Palisades. She even gets them clothes, traveling all the way downtown and to Brooklyn to find better discounts in clothing and shoe stores. Hers is just about the only 'mothering' class in the system. We could use a lot more."

We were back in the corridor. Mrs. LaBeet had an appointment with a parent. The roles of guidance counselors are diverse, particularly at P.S. 119. They work on an individual basis with children who have special problems; they help get supplementary welfare payments for parents and intervene in their dealings with other agencies; they ease the entry of open-enrollment transfers from P.S. 119 to other schools; they're involved with testing; they counsel new teachers and are available for advice to veteran teachers; and they work with parents. "I keep believing," Mrs. LaBeet said in farewell, "that one day it'll be better. It's getting harder to believe that, but maybe—" She walked away.

III

When I came into the principal's office the next day, John was operating a Thermofax machine. Shapiro handed him a letter. "Two copies, please," he said to the boy. "It's a very important letter."

We went into Shapiro's own office. On a table was a bag of grass seed. "There was another bag," he said. "I gave it to John a couple of weeks ago when he asked for it. For a while he held it in his arms like a rag doll, rocking it back and forth. Then he thought he might plant the seeds in the park. Later he said he might put them on his mother's grave. And he gave me a little box of dirt with one of the grass seeds in it. I was very proud of it and kept it on my desk, but we had a hot argument one day and in his anger, he took the box and spilled everything into the wastepaper basket.

"But he's coming along. He did rip down some posters in the hall this morning, and he's been stealing a bit of money from the office. But sometimes, when a child steals, he steals from a person he likes. The fantasy is that the person has given him a gift because he likes him. I learned that when I was working with disturbed children at Bellevue years ago. I'd been working day after day with a boy who had serious reading difficulties. One day he stole my watch. I felt destroyed, like a martyred parent. But fortunately, Dr. Lauretta Bender, a child psychiatrist on the staff, explained what was happening, and it did turn out the theft had actually been a mark of affection."

John came in with the copies. "Fine." Shapiro looked at them. "Make me another one."

"Make up your mind," said John.

"I apologize," Shapiro said, smiling. John grinned and went out with the letter.

In an hour, Shapiro told me, there was to be a meeting of the school's parents' association in the teachers' room. I mentioned that Mrs. LaBeet had told me the P.S. 119 Parents' Association was an aggressive one, although one of the stereotypes about schools in neighborhoods of the poor is that it's difficult to get parents involved in such groups.

"Well"—Shapiro leaned back—"for a long time it was difficult here too. The parents didn't trust us and they had good reason not to. One of the problems with parents in this kind of neighborhood is supposed to be that they're nonverbal. But they often have very good reasons for not saying much to school administrators. They're thinking, 'Why don't the children have readers to take home and why don't they have more of other things too?' But often the parents don't ask, because they sense the principal is loyal to the system and not to the children, and they figure 'What's the use? He's not going to do anything to change the system.' So it's an act of intelligence on their part to refuse to enter into what would be a phony dialogue.

"Here the parents were slow to accept that we were talking

honestly about the deficiencies of the school. We told them that what we were doing was much impaired because we didn't have the resources to do very much. That kind of admission was something new in their experience. We admitted, for example, that we didn't have enough books, and finally we got the parents to write to the Board and ask for more. Between their efforts and ours we did get more, and then we discovered that many of the same parents who had seemed inarticulate were very verbal and quite sophisticated. We began with only ten parents coming to meetings, but eventually we were getting seven hundred and fifty at important meetings. The other day the room was so full that I, one of the speakers, had to stand in the hall.

"However, there's always a residue of criticism of our school. When I first came, I began to relax the discipline in the school—in the narrow sense of that word—and there were parents who interpreted that action as indicating I was just another white man who didn't care about their children. If I cared, I'd discipline them more. I think we've proved we do care, but there are still parents who feel our discipline isn't strong enough. They go off to work and are worried about their children being alone. So the threat of severe corporal punishment if the child misbehaves is always in the air, almost like a wireless between the parent and the child. They want us to 'protect' the child in the same way they do. I keep telling them it would actually be easier for us to use strong discipline—in that narrow sense—but that our staff tries to develop the children's liveliness. Being 'good' in a rigid sense gets in the way of learning. The child begins to give the teacher only what the teacher wants and loses his appetite for learning, his curiosity, and part of his identity.

"We're trying to help them develop an *inner* discipline. A child must have enough energy left in him to remain courageous. By that I mean the ability to question rather than always saying, 'Yes, sir,' and 'No, sir.' I think it's good that many of our children are able to question the wisdom of the adults in this building. It's particularly important for Negro children. They've been taught it's safe to be respectful. We want them to understand that they're citizens and they *can* question. That is, they're citizens except for one right—the right not to go to school. It's a very important right, and since we've taken it away from them, it's our responsibility to make the school as interesting as possible. You know, at Junior High School 136, where many of our children go when they leave here, our kids are considered outstanding in behavior in that they're not hostile to the teachers. Being able to question them, they can respect and trust them.

"The children in Mr. Marcus's fifth-grade class, incidentally," Shapiro said with evident satisfaction, "have been doing some important questioning. They analyzed a sizable number of social studies textbooks and they found every one to be wanting. Then they wrote letters to the publishers and to some of the people in the school system pointing out that certain matters of opinion were being treated as facts. The statement in one book, for example, that on the whole, the slaves were happy on the plantations. The children got many replies, and not being satisfied with some of them, they wrote again."

I asked Shapiro what the reaction had been from on high in the school system.

He smiled. "There were inquiries. Nothing was said that was an outright condemnation, but implicit in the questions was: 'How could you let this happen?' Among the inquiries were: 'What kinds of lessons are being given in that social studies class? Was the teacher biased? Did you discuss this project with the children? Perhaps there were better textbooks in the catalogue that were not analyzed?' Those are the kinds of questions that keep teachers passive. My answer was that at this point there is no social studies textbook which treats the Negro fairly, and that the children's questions were a true culmination of their research and were an excellent learning experience.

"Another residue of criticism from the parents," Shapiro continued, "is that the children aren't achieving well enough. It's obvious to some parents of sixth-grade children, for instance, that their kids are not reading at sixth-grade level. Some say, 'Why don't you hold the child back?' We do hold some back, but we don't have the facilities to do much good if we were to keep a lot of them back. And we do have Reading Improvement Teachers who take small groups out of the classroom for remedial reading work and who also work with teachers inside the classroom by concentrating on a particular group and leaving the teacher free to focus on the rest of the class. We do more of that than most schools. But we don't have enough teachers and small enough classes to do all that has to be done. The parents have a very real grievance. Two-thirds of our children in the sixth grade are not reading at grade level. That's better than ninety-nine per cent when I came, but it's hardly a triumph. If every teacher in the school were superior, we'd be able to reduce that proportion to one-third—even with big classes. But the human race being what it is, it's impossible to get that many superior teachers, just as it's impossible to find that many superior doctors, psychiatrists, and engineers. Therefore, we have to make conditions for teaching so good that the average teacher can become effective. If the context for teaching is superior, the average teacher will do as well as a superior teacher would have done in a bad setting."

Miss Jones, the assistant principal in charge of the lower grades, came in. With her was a young second-grade teacher. "Exciting news!" said Miss Jones, pointing to the teacher. "Thirteen in her class have finished *Our New Friends.*" The teacher beamed. "That's only a first-grade book, of course, but Gus is really reading. He's picked up lots of new words." The teacher left. "That's when we get the rewards." Miss Jones turned to me. "You feel you're up against a blank wall, and suddenly one day light dawns and the child unfolds. No wonder a teacher feels like shouting when that happens. And you have no idea of the months of energy and effort that went into getting Gus to read. They didn't nickname him 'Granite Gus' for nothing."

"That sort of thing gets through to the parents too," said Shapiro. "I mean the great emotional investment our teachers have in getting the children to learn. The depth of that kind of concern only becomes clear over a long period of time, but once it was made evident in a very dramatic way."

IV

Shapiro was referring to "the incident of the rat" at P.S. 119, an event that briefly made the school famous and had more than a little to do with the construction of P.S. 92 as a replacement for it. "Five years ago," he explained, "the physical conditions here were awful. The plaster was falling down. When it rained, there were floods in the halls. And there was no way to get the building clean with all the vermin and cockroaches around. You could run into a rat on any floor. I sent letters and letters to the Board and to the assistant superintendent in charge of this district. No answers. I'd call and be told, 'It's not my department. I'll switch you.' I'd hold on and nothing would happen. Some of the parents went to City Hall to show pictures of water running in the halls. Still nothing happened. We had a number of staff meetings, trying to figure out what to do. Finally, I suggested that we could always advertise in the newspaper. Everybody chipped in, and on May 22, 1961, an ad appeared on the school page of the *World Telegram.*" He rummaged through his files and showed me the ad:

HELP!   HELP!   HELP!

HELP US TO GET A NEW SCHOOL TO

SAVE OUR CHILDREN

GIVE US A BUILDING WITHOUT

1. *Rats and Roaches on Every Floor*
2. *A Leaking Roof*
3. *Broken Door Frames*
4. *Split Sessions (½ an education)*
5. *Refrigerator Temperatures in the Winter and Oven-Like Sweltering During Spring*
6. *Irreparable Plumbing, Resulting In: Backups, Leaks, Flooded Yards and Corridors and Lunchrooms*
7. *Sagging, Dangerous Walls*
8. *Overcrowding in Lunchrooms and Classrooms*
9. *Unsanitary Children's Toilets*
10. *Wasteful Temporary Patching of Obsolete and Intrinsically Inadequate Scrap-Pile Facilities Without Shoving The Taxpayers Money Down The Drain*
11. *Condemnation of Nine Classrooms of Our Old (1899) School Where Our Entire Building Is Wrought with Fire and Health Hazards*

OUR CHILDREN DESERVE

A NEW SCHOOL

NOW!!

The Teaching, clerical and administrative staff of Public School #119—Manhattan

"That was the first time in the history of the New York Public School System," Shapiro grinned, "anything like that had happened."

The ad appeared on a Monday, and there was no word from the Board for the next few days. Shapiro's interpretation of the silence was that "no one dared to be the first to call us up because then it would be *his* responsibility to find out what had gone wrong." Radio and television stations, newspapers and newsmagazines, however, picked up the story. The persistent Gabe Pressman of WNBC-TV arrived at the school, saw four rats, had them chased with a camera, and was exacerbated at their reluctance to be photographed. At eleven o'clock on Thursday night of that week, Shapiro was telephoned at home by a man who called him "Elliott" and who identified himself as the Mayor's educational representative. Shapiro had never heard of him before. The Mayor, Shapiro was informed, was going to visit the school next day with the president of the Board of Education and several high administrative officials of the school system. His educational representative wanted to know the physical layout of P.S. 119 so that the route of the Mayor's tour could be planned.

The next morning, Mayor Robert Wagner arrived. As Shapiro ushered the Mayor and the school officials into the auditorium, a teacher and several students suddenly pointed vigorously at a corner of the room and yelled, "Rat!" Seizing a broom which was kept in the corner for rat-chasing, the principal pursued the rodent. The Mayor, somewhat shaken, peered in the direction of the hunt but wasn't quick enough to see the rat before it escaped under a radiator. The rathole, however, was visible.

After the Mayor left, Shapiro returned to his office and found an angry associate superintendent waiting for him.

"Why didn't you go through channels?" he demanded of Shapiro. "This is a hell of a thing—airing our dirty linen in public. Ellie, you're disgracing us! This should have been kept a family affair."

"We did try all possible channels," Shapiro answered calmly, "and there were no results."

"Sure," the associate superintendent said sardonically, "you chose an effective method to publicize your grievances. But you could have been just as effective by burning down the building."

Shapiro didn't answer. "I forgave him that first outburst," he later recalled, "because he was chagrined." But the associate superintendent repeated his analogy of the newspaper ad and the burning down of the school.

"No," Shapiro said softly, "the two are not equivalent. What we did was simply part of the democratic process as it applies to education. After appealing through channels, we owed it to the public to let it know what was happening. Your talking about burning down the building indicates that you and we have radically different concepts of the democratic process. And I'll be glad to debate you on it any time and any place."

"We'll do that," the associate superintendent said grimly. "Where would you suggest?"

"In front of Dr. Theobald." Dr. John Theobald, then Superintendent of Schools, was in Europe at the time investigating the school systems of various countries.

"I don't think," Shapiro laughed, "that he'd be an entirely impartial audience."

Dour, the associate superintendent left. In addition to the Mayor and representatives of the school-system hierarchy, there had been other visitors at P.S. 119 that day, including parents of pupils and officers of several unions whom Shapiro had contacted. "If the Mayor's visit had boomeranged," Shapiro told me, "we would have had more than a thousand pickets at the school the next Monday and there would have been pressure from the labor movement on certain politicians.

In a sense, it's too bad it didn't boomerang. I felt that the picketing would have been a good educational experience for the children—and their parents too."

Exterminators worked at the school during the Memorial Day weekend. They fumigated the premises and killed forty rats. In July of 1961, Dr. Theobald, back from Europe, charged that the "incident of the rat" had been "a cleverly handled public relations stunt." He had found no one, Theobald told the press, who had seen the rat.

When newspaper reporters called him, Shapiro answered that "two teachers and a large number of children had seen the rat" and that he had many witnesses who had seen many other rats. The reporters returned to Theobald. He allowed that perhaps there had been a rat in sight that day but called the incident "a tempest in a teapot," adding that "there is no question there were rats in the building. The neighborhood is loaded with rats. It was the specific incident I had doubts about."

Soon Shapiro received a telephone call, "Hello, Elliott, this is John."

"John who?" Informed it was the Superintendent of Schools, Shapiro whispered to a friend, "Our greatest enemies call us by our first names." The call was to summon Shapiro to a meeting. They had been in the same room before at a meeting of school supervisory personnel, but this was the first personal dialogue between them. Shapiro told the Superintendent that all the way up the chain of command in the school system were people with a vested interest in keeping the truth away from the person on the next rung up. By the time anything came to the top, Shapiro observed, conditions were reported as being fine. "In a sense"—he looked at Theobald—"your difficulty is somewhat like that of a soldier walking in a territory that has been mined but in which everyone else has concealed the possibility of an explosion."

Theobald, however, kept concentrating on the rat, repeating he had no evidence that one had actually been present during the Mayor's visit.

"Well," said Shapiro, after telling of his witnesses, "the exterminators did kill forty of them right afterward."

Theobald looked at Shapiro stonily. "Thirty-nine," he said.

The building, in any case, had remained in disrepair and it had been expected that workmen would rehabilitate P.S. 119 during that summer. Nothing happened. On the first day of school in September, an army of laborers arrived and started breaking down doors and walls. The dust was pervasive and the plaster was in motion. The schoolyard, moreover, was being torn up, and piles of rubble effectively prevented its use by the children. The parents, indignant, decided to act, met with Shapiro, and set up a picket line protesting the fact that the school was unsafe. A corollary boycott was called, and for two days, nine hundred children were absent. It was the most successful boycott of a New York City public school up to that point. "I couldn't tell them to keep their children out," Shapiro says of his role in the boycott, "but they knew I was empathic."

On the second day of the picketing, leaders of the Parents' Association were meeting with Dr. Theobald at Board headquarters in Brooklyn. Shapiro was about to leave for that meeting when a Rolls Royce stopped at the door of P.S. 119. A member of the Board of Education stepped out, and in a few minutes was joined by two other Board members. It had started to rain, but the line of picketing parents remained firm. The Board members went up to Shapiro's office on the second floor. They asked Shapiro to invite the pickets to join them upstairs and discuss whether there actually was a need to picket. Shapiro relayed the message. The answer was: "We appreciate the Board members' having come, but we would prefer they meet us on the same level in the lunchroom on the ground floor." And there the meeting was held.

"It was a great experience," says Shapiro. "That request did not come from parents who were leaders. But the pickets were astute enough not to go up to authority. Their choice of the lunchroom was symbolic. They were saying, 'Meet us on a down-to-earth level. If we go upstairs, we're on your ground.'"

The meeting was inconclusive, and later that day Shapiro went to Brooklyn, arriving a little before the meeting of Theobald and other school officials with the leaders of the Parents' Association broke up. The president of the Parents' Association invited an associate superintendent—the same official who had been incensed at the ad in the *World Tele-gram*—to visit the school the next day. At first he demurred but finally said he would come the following night. When he arrived, seven hundred and fifty parents were there to greet him despite the shortness of time there had been to alert the parent body. The meeting was held in the inner yard on the ground floor. From his demeanor the previous day, the associate superintendent, Shapiro expected, had planned to deliver a stern lecture to the parents. Seeing so many of them, his tone softened. He told them he welcomed their interest in the school, but he could not resist adding a short homily urging them to send their children to class in as well prepared a manner as possible—with clean shirts and shoes. The parents, feeling they already did that, were more interested in when the school would be fit for their children to attend.

An agreement was finally reached with school officials by which fifth- and sixth-grade students were temporarily moved to other schools, thereby emptying a rotating series of classrooms for the laborers to work in. In addition, the Board reluctantly agreed to pay time and a half for work done after three in the afternoon and on Saturdays so that the school's rehabilitation would be further quickened.

V

The incident of the rat and the parents' boycott did not make Dr. Shapiro's relationship with his superiors any warmer than it had been. One morning I asked him to estimate his status at 110 Livingston Street in Brooklyn, the Board's headquarters. "I would say," he said drily, "that for a long period, it has been recognized that my opinions are often different from those of the Board of Education, some headquarters personnel, and the Council of Supervisory Associations, to which most of the other principals belong. I have regard for the Board of Education, but it has never fully recognized that it ought to be functioning as the representative of the children. All children, but most particularly poor children who have the fewest representatives to power. The Board should make strong, continual statements about the urgent need for money and services. They should organize their energies in much more dramatic ways. So far the Board has represented education in a taxpayers' style. Instead they ought to keep haranguing the city to the point at which a real exploration takes place of how to get the essential funds. A change in the tax structure, for one way. Taxation from real estate now accounts for a much smaller proportion of city revenues than ever before in history. They have to carry the fight to the State and Federal governments, not just petition. Sure, there'd be some complaints from parts of the citizenry, but it's useful to get those complaints out in the open. And the middle class as a whole would not really oppose this kind of push. The middle is always passive. Alienated from its own beliefs, it doesn't know it has beliefs until things are stirred up. We have to make education *the* basic industry in this city.

"Specifically," Shapiro said, "if we could extend the school budget by some four hundred million dollars a year—and that's not much—we could reduce class size significantly. Oh, it's a sizable sum, but consider it in the context of a municipal budget that is over *four billion dollars* a year! For only sixty million dollars a year, we could make every elementary school—and perhaps the junior high schools too—in Harlem, the South Bronx, Jamaica, and Bedford-Stuyvesant a qualitatively effective school. In Harlem, it would take six to seven million dollars more a year to make the twenty elementary and junior high schools into qualitatively effective schools. It certainly can't be impossible to get that kind of money."

I mentioned to Shapiro that on the previous Sunday I had heard an assistant superintendent of schools, in a speech to Harlem parents on radio station WLIB, say that "Educationally, we have nothing to be ashamed of here in Harlem."

"It was an honest opinion," Shapiro said, "and it's shared by many people in the system. They mean that they're doing about the best they can with the present resources. But they

fail to recognize that resources are not so limited as they
have taken them to be. We ought to be ashamed—I mean
those of us in the school system—that we have not been
leaders for dramatic improvements and that we do participate in a process in which two-thirds—or maybe three-
fourths—of the children are being so badly undereducated
that we're giving them a lifetime of unemployment.

"Let me give you another example of how all of us have
been dropouts as educators," Shapiro went on. "For years, we
gave children in neighborhoods like this reading tests—
geared to the experiences of middle-class children—and we
used those tests as indices of the children's intelligence quo-
tients. The result was a self-fulfilling prophecy. The children,
the theory ran, were reading poorly because they were
stupid. Consider the insensitivity of the educators in charge.
We were torturing the kids with those tests and we were
tormenting the teachers as well. Yet no group of principals
or of headquarters personnel criticized that technique of
demeaning the children. Of course, we had a kind of vested
interest in not complaining about the way we were testing
them. If you accept the premise that these children have
low I. Q.s, according to the national average, our own woe-
ful inefficiency doesn't come out. Only in the past couple of
years, as a result of pressure from the civil rights movement, have we stopped giving those standardized, middle-
class-biased I. Q. tests. Now we're giving them achievement
tests in various subject areas. They too remain middle-class-
biased, but at least they're used to judge the child's achievement level rather than as an index of his native endowment
of intelligence.

"Why do we have tests?" Shapiro answered his question:
"Primarily because we don't have enough personnel. If we
had enough personnel, we'd have sufficient understanding
of each child in depth and we'd see the test results as they

really are—embryonic in a very rudimentary sense." I asked Dr. Shapiro's reaction to a recent statement by Harold Taylor, a former president of Sarah Lawrence College: "We have more tests than we can use now. We test for the wrong things . . . standardized testing paralyzes thinking. Let's throw all the tests out, abolish them, and concentrate on teaching."

Shapiro nodded approvingly. "But," he added, "if we do give tests, let's give them on a one-to-one basis. One child to each tester. That way the test would involve real communication between the tester and the child. If a test is being given to a group of thirty, how can one tester know which children are daydreaming that morning and which didn't have any breakfast?

"There's so much more that can be done besides radically revising testing procedures and getting smaller classes. Take this neighborhood. It's poor. Stores go out of business, leaving many vacant storefronts—some with backyards—that could be used as classrooms. From 110th to 145th Streets and between Seventh and Eighth Avenues, there are the equivalent of forty to fifty potential classrooms. Why not use them primarily for young children—with the backyards as schoolyards, and with libraries interspersed here and there? The libraries could be for parents as well as children and could be open until eight or nine in the evening. We would be coming right into the heart of the community, creating the kind of reciprocal relationship between the community and the schools that you don't find anywhere in this city—or in the country. We'd be on constant display, and people would be welcome to come in and see what we're doing. And if they wanted to, they could help as parent aides. The plan would take care of classroom shortages and would represent *real* decentralization. It could be a stimulus toward the creation of a new society. But we couldn't have an adult-to-pupil ratio of one to twenty-eight in those storefront schools. That way it couldn't be made interesting enough so that the kids would be eager to come. The classes would have to be quite small.

"I've proposed this idea to the Board, with the estimate that it would take $4,000 to transform each vacant store into a classroom. The Board's estimate was $10,000, but even $10,000 isn't that much money when you consider that the average classroom in a regular school costs more than $60,-000 to construct."

I mentioned that Shapiro had yet to talk about ways to integrate the schools. "To begin with," he said, "the storefront classrooms could increase the possibilities of integration. As you spread out along the avenues, you would break through district lines and move into neighborhoods that would allow for different racial balances in those classrooms. There are other ways too. Often segregation is on an economic basis. Segregation of black and white is more obvious in appearance, but look at what we have in Harlem. Increasingly fewer middle-class parents—those, for instance, in Lenox Terrace or the Riverton Houses—send their children to public schools. Take P.S. 197. It's in a largely middle-class Negro community, and its teachers are the equivalent of those in the private schools, but hardly any of those middle-class parents send their children there. We—I mean teachers—have to begin by leafleting and by approaching these parents and other middle-class parents, both Negro and white, in other ways, to make an issue of this. Of course, simultaneously, the public schools in Harlem have to be made much more effective. At present, it may be that a middle-class child, Negro or white, isn't sufficiently challenged in a class of thirty made up largely of kids at lower levels of achievement. But in a class of twelve or fifteen, children coming from different backgrounds would have a lot to offer each other. Certainly if the class size at P.S. 197 were around ten, those middle-class parents would send their children there.

"As for outside of Harlem, granted that in the city as a whole, more than fifty per cent of the children in the first grades are now nonwhite. If things go on as they have been, it will be harder and harder to find schools to integrate with. But if the schools are drastically improved throughout the city, particularly in our neighborhoods, I'm convinced more and more middle-class parents—Negro and white alike—will return their children to public school. And if children are to be bussed out of their own neighborhoods, it will be to a first-rate school, thereby changing the nature of *that* discussion. Right now, all through the city, children are being picked up to travel to private schools where there's more personal involvement with the teachers. Why can't the public schools do this?

"In Harlem and in other poor neighborhoods," Shapiro added, "we can have some of our schools emphasize certain specialties—the new math, say, or language arts. On an elementary school level, they could be beacons—like the Bronx High School of Science. There are white parents who would send their children to those schools. It's been happening for years at the High School of Music and Art at the edge of Harlem. There are schools here only ten minutes from Washington Heights by station wagon. I've talked to groups of parents in Washington Heights. On the whole, they were opposed to bussing, but when I told them about *this* kind of possibility, they were eager to try it. A school of quality obviously can fulfill one of a parent's status needs as well as his educational desires for his children. Neighborhoods in which the poorest people live, those who are most discriminated against, should get those status schools first, and the middle class would come. That was a mistake the Board made when they tried pairing schools. The Board didn't dramatically enough improve the schools in the poor neighborhoods that were involved."

As we talked further about integrating the schools, we moved out of Shapiro's office because it was time for him to put a dime in the parking meter. "As this goes on—the storefront classrooms and the beacon schools—those middle-class Negro parents who want to leave Harlem," he said, "should be encouraged to move into white neighborhoods, thereby bringing more integration outside the ghettos. For one thing, the Board of Education ought to make it a policy that principals in white neighborhoods take on leadership in encouraging the invitation of Negro families into those areas. On the whole, the principals of this city are good-hearted, but to get them involved in this kind of action would require its being official policy. Then they'd go along."

I asked him about educational parks as a way to accelerate city-wide public school integration. These large complexes of schools would range from the early grades through high school. Set up in central locations, they could serve wide areas and transcend neighborhood boundaries. "It's a good principle," Shapiro answered. "You can more economically make available the best possible facilities rather than having to stretch out second-rate facilities in neighborhood schools. But I begin to be concerned when the plan for an educational park is so big that I envision buses stretching for miles and miles. But if the educational park is not too vast, it could make sense. We could have had one right in this neighborhood if the Board hadn't decided to move the High School of Music and Art from Convent Avenue into Lincoln Center. Music and Art could have been lined up with five elementary schools, including 119, and the junior high school at 135th Street and St. Nicholas Avenue. City College is near by and we could have drawn on their reservoir of specialists."

As we walked through the schoolyard, Shapiro waved at a thin, well-dressed, middle-aged Negro across the street. "The local numbers broker," he remarked. "Some of these basic improvements," he went on, "can be put in motion by teachers spurring the parents. In our neighborhoods, action for beacon schools, smaller classes, educational parks can start that way. You know, it's very often said that the schools reflect the social order. Actually that often means the schools are institutions of apology for the social order. But it doesn't have to be that way. The schools could be an instrument for changing the social order into a more truly democratic society. But for that to happen we have to break the circle in which professional personnel tend to remain loyal to institutions rather than to the human beings who should be served by those institutions. And we have to do much more than restrict our appeals to higher echelons within those institutions. Take finances again. The usual method of appealing for funds is cyclic. The appeals go round and round through the same channels, fiscal year after fiscal year, and only when a scandal occurs is direct contact made with the public. Only then is the public made to feel the urgency of the need. This method is not only self-defeating but is also basically undemocratic. The result is that the potential of the children remains untapped, that of poor children especially, and the community as a whole is kept ignorant as to what *could* happen. So, since our first loyalty—as teachers—should be to the child, it's our responsibility, if appeals through channels keep going astray, to make direct contact with the public ourselves."

VI

We returned to the school. It was time to welcome actor-playwright Ossie Davis, who had been invited by the staff civil rights committee to address an assembly of the fifth and sixth grades. Accompanied by a Nigerian, who was working as a reporter for the *New York Amsterdam News*, the tall, deep-voiced, graying Davis was escorted to the auditorium on the fourth floor. On a bulletin board near the entrance to the auditorium was a poster announcing the coming of an African dance troupe on the evening of May 26, under the sponsorship of the Parents' Association of P.S. 119. Inside, I was given a program for this morning's event. Listed were the poems and songs to be performed by the children, and at the bottom was a line ascribed to Ossie Davis: "Man is indeed a giant, but who is to tell him so?" Above it was the note: "Ruby Dee is a former student of P.S. 119—Manhattan." Over the stage was a sign in black paint on white paper: TO FACE THE FUTURE WE MUST KNOW OUR PAST.

From a window at the back of the hall I looked at grimy tenements; old, rotting apartment houses; cans full of uncollected garbage; and shops, including an abandoned grocery store. Eight children were singing:

> "Get on board, little children,
> And fight for human rights.
> We may go to jail
> But if we fight for freedom
> There's no such thing as bail."

Dr. Shapiro introduced Ossie Davis. "Now that he is known throughout the country," the principal said, "it would be easy for this wonderful actor and playwright to separate himself from us. But the more widely recognized he becomes, the more he involves himself with everyone striving for freedom."

Davis immediately seized and kept the children's attention. He acted out pungent poems by Langston Hughes and Gwendolyn Brooks, along with some of his own, and climaxed his performance with a highly mobile recitation of "Casey at the Bat." Davis gave way to a sixth grader, Cleveland Bumpers, who read his own poem, "Negroes and Whites":

> "Negroes and whites should have equal rights
> Instead of judging each other and having a fight.
> Negroes and whites should not disagree.
> Everyone in the world should be free.
> Why are Negroes and whites having a fight?
> Is it because whites are light?
> Why are Negroes so mad?
> Is it because they are treated so bad?
> When everyone in the world is free,
> There will be none to disagree."

Davis rose again and told the children that he had greatly enjoyed his time with them. "When I was a boy in Waycross, Georgia," he added, smiling, "we had speakers too and we wanted them to talk with us for a long time so that we'd get all their wisdom and not have to go back to the classroom. Why, we had one man, a dentist, who'd just say, 'Brush your teeth,' and we'd applaud him." The children laughed.

"What I want to see"—Davis grew serious—"is all integrated schools with all different kinds of children because we have so many things to tell each other about ourselves. I'd like to know what makes Irishmen proud to be Irish and what in the history of the Jews is particularly pleasing to the Jews. I already know the things that make me proud of my people, and I'd like others to know them too. The other thing I want to say to you is make the most of your opportunities here.

"You know my wife, Ruby Dee?" Many of the children nodded, and a few applauded. "Well, she went to this school and what she got out of it helped make her a great actress. If it happened to her, it could happen to you. Suppose you want to be an actor. You have to know English so you can speak your lines, and you have to know arithmetic so you won't be cheated at the end of the week. And you need discipline so you can do what the director wants. All this you get here free, and in this school, you have teachers who care."

The children were getting restive, but Davis recaptured their attention by starting to sing "We Shall Overcome." Everyone stood and joined in, including Shapiro. As Davis began to leave, there were cries of "Oh, no!" and "More!" He agreed to do a final poem. It ended:

"There are words like liberty that almost make me cry.
If you had known what I've known, you'd know why."

"Isn't that so?" he asked the audience. There was applause, followed by a surge of children asking for his autograph. A girl broke through the crowd to present Davis with a bouquet of flowers for his wife. On the outskirts of the wriggling mob was John, brooding. Shapiro tried to joke with him, but John moved away. A few minutes later, Shapiro introduced John to Ossie Davis. "This boy wants to be a writer."

"Will you write a poem or a story I might see?" Davis asked him.

John shrugged his shoulders.

"Make me a promise. Write a poem and I'll ask your teacher to send it to me."

John made no promise, but he did hold out a program to be autographed. As Davis signed, John allowed himself a smile.

Miss Carmen Jones had moved alongside Davis. "This boy"—she looked at John—"can do almost anything he wants to. He has great ability."

Shapiro, at a distance, was watching. "John's very pleased to have met Davis," Shapiro told me, "but for a while he's going to have to treat it negatively. Part of his own self-devaluation. Besides, he's been bugged since yesterday. I'm not sure about what; but at least, unlike a few months ago, he's not shouting and throwing things. He's on a new plateau."

Davis went to visit some of the classrooms and was accompanied by Shapiro. In one, a shy girl asked the actor about stage fright. "You do get that," said Davis, "but the thing is not to be ashamed. You have to have the courage to go out on stage and say, 'Here I am. I like me. I hope you like me too.'" The girl giggled. As Davis left the classroom, the children crowded around him for autographs. The teacher frowned, but Shapiro whispered to her, "I don't think he minds, and the children *want* this closeness."

In the corridor, a chunky girl came up to Shapiro. She was close to tears. "My leg hurts," she said. "It's that terrible scab here on my knee." Shapiro waved Davis on and stayed with the girl.

"Bend it."

"I can't," she said.

"Come." He took her by the hand and walked her to her classroom. "If it still hurts after class," he said at the door, "you come in to see me."

"That girl," Shapiro said, "is a bit of a faker. She's using that scab for some reason right now. I'll find out about it later."

We joined Davis in Mrs. Taylor's classroom. The initial reaction of the children to him was much more muted than it had been in the previous room. "Mrs. Taylor," Shapiro said softly to Davis, "protects these children. That's why they're here. But she also believes in strong discipline, and when a class is this disciplined, the kids won't express curiosity readily." Davis nodded. In a few minutes the children were more openly star-struck, and one, a slender, attractive girl of about twelve, read Davis a poem she had written.

"She," Shapiro said to me, "has two older brothers. One is in jail and the other is doing all he can to emulate his older brother. The girl used to act out her aggressions often, but she's been quite happy since she's been with Mrs. Taylor. She's been protected."

As we walked to another room, Davis noticed the pictures of Africa and a series of African folk tales on a bulletin board. "We're trying," Shapiro told him, "to integrate Afro-American culture into the curriculum all year round. Not just during Negro History Week."

We crossed through the gym, where the noise was so overpowering that only shouted conversation could be heard. I noticed a heavy-set boy of about thirteen following Shapiro doggedly. "You'll get your basketball back," Shapiro yelled above the din, "but I don't want to make it too easy for you."

The boy turned away. "Hey," Shapiro shouted after him, "if anybody picks on you, let me know."

We left the gym. Walking behind Davis, Shapiro said, "That was Duncan. I'm almost afraid that boy's doomed. He's not a smart boy, but he is perhaps the strongest boy in the school. There may be an aphasic problem there, but in any case, it's very hard to deal with him. His home situation is very bad. He acts as if he wants *something*, anything to happen to him. Something different from what he knows. He's even told me he wants to get into some kind of institution. Now that's unusual. A while ago, we had a stream of girls coming to the office complaining that he had hit them. I sent Mrs. LaBeet to his mother to ask if I could hit *him*. On the shoulder. Lightly. Just to show him I could.

"Unfortunately, the mother was all too willing to agree. She'd have let me use a stick. But I did shove him lightly so he'd know I was strong enough—in his terms—to take care of him. And that's also why I said that just now about his letting me know if anyone picked on him. Actually he's the one who picks on the littler children. This morning he pulled a knife which we took away along with the basketball. But, by my saying that to him now, he may get the feeling he's protected. Duncan and I seem to be on better terms these days. Now he'll even smile sometimes. But after here, where is the boy to go? Where can he get sustained psychotherapy more than once a week? And as for institutionalizing him for observation, the institutions are all overcrowded with long waiting lists. So he's almost *got* to get into trouble sooner or later. There just aren't the facilities. Not enough facilities for the disturbed, and not enough facilities to educate those who are not disturbed. One possibility for Duncan is a 600 School, if he could be put in a very small class with a man teacher. But there's such a tremendous waiting list for the 600 Schools too."

Shapiro quickened his pace. "I have gotten Duncan to promise that when he begins to feel very angry because he's picked on or because he *feels* he's being picked on, he'll come to me before he hits anyone. But he doesn't always keep that promise."

We passed a kindergarten class. Shapiro looked in the door for a moment. "That teacher," he said, "is so well organized that she's organized the room rather than the children. She's much too distant from them. She's not *physically* close enough to them. I usually have a certain amount of autonomy as to what teachers I can get rid of, but it's limited."

Ossie Davis visited two more classes before going into the teachers' room for lunch with the staff and some of the parents. I recognized a woman I'd seen nearly every time I'd been at the school and asked her if she were on the staff. "No," she smiled. "I'm a parent, and I work with the Parents' Association. Sometimes I do feel as if I'm on the staff, though. I feel so at home. I feel with him"—she nodded in the direction of Shapiro—"that I can walk into his office any time. You don't have to make appointments."

She joined a half dozen other mothers who were concerned that, although the new school was nearly finished, a series of substantial repairs had been ordered for P.S. 119.

"We have to get this building *down*," one mother said to Shapiro, who had joined their group. "The children will need this space for a yard."

"It is very odd," said Shapiro. "On the one hand, we keep getting assurances that 119 will be torn down as soon as 92 is finished. But on the other hand, they're investing quite a lot in these repairs. However, don't underestimate the surrealistic irrationality of the school system. They could very well fix this place up and then tear it down. But we have to make sure."

As Ossie Davis signed autographs, the mothers, several

teachers and Shapiro were devising letters to the Board and planning on the most effective ways in which to enlist their local assemblyman and other public officials to whom they had access.

"What," asked one parent, "if we get no more answers at all from Livingston Street?"

"Oh," said Mrs. Zelma West, a trim, forceful guidance counselor and a remarkable energizer of the community, "they'll answer. They know us down there. But the thing is to give them a deadline."

"I heard," a large, angry woman said, "that they had already given out a new two-year custodial contract for this school. They may plan to use 119 for adult rehabilitation and vocational retraining."

"I've heard that rumor too," said Shapiro, "and we have to check it out. But again, it wouldn't be out of character for the Board to allot the contract and still tear down the building."

They began to work on the wording of the letter to the Board.

"Assurances were given us."

"Yes, get that in. If the building stands, we are being betrayed."

"And make sure you put in," said a teacher, "that if we get no satisfaction from them, we'll take the issue to the community."

"End it: 'May we expect your reply immediately?' "

"How about," Shapiro suggested, " 'May we be favored with a reply as soon as possible, because this topic will be the basis of the agenda for our very next meeting?' "

"And say when that meeting is."

"And invite them down to it," added Shapiro.

"Anyway," Mrs. West ended the discussion, "get ready to picket, so that if we have to demonstrate, they'll be confronted with a sea of faces. If you have to bring the little ones, bring them. After all, you're buying their future."

The group moved to where Davis was sitting, surrounded by staff members and parents. "It sounds presumptuous," he was saying between sips of coffee, "for me to come from the outside and speak with authority on how you should run your school, but there are some similarities between what I do and what you do. When real communication is established between a teacher and a child, there's a quality of excitement in the acquisition of knowledge that resembles what takes place in the highest forms of theatrical experience. There are plays in which the actor—through the writer—builds a character to the point of discovering something about himself he didn't know before. A discovery that changes his life.

"Well," Davis continued, "as a child learns more about who he is, *you* have the key role in his expanding and understanding that knowledge. In the old days, when the family was much more central to all areas of human experience, the mother and father could stimulate and clarify that growing self-image. Now, for many reasons, the family is fragmented; and in this neighborhood, the family is often practically destroyed. So you have that job. You have to *be* there when the child has the need to define himself with regard to his culture and his background. Give the child material to show him who he is, but you also have to love and understand that material. Our history as Negroes is more than our coming here as slaves and just surviving. There are strengths in our past that the young Negro child ought to have a chance to identify with. If he doesn't, he may become unteachable. You can't just talk about the universality of man. First you need knowledge of and pride in your own culture. And then you go on to discover that at the core of every distinct culture are the common imperatives of all men."

"Uh-*huh!*" a Negro teacher said emphatically in agreement. Others, including Shapiro, were nodding vigorously.

"The pride I feel in myself and my past," said Davis, "is not a defensive pride. It's open and welcoming because I was able to learn to love myself. After that I was able to try to learn to love the rest of this country."

Davis looked at his watch, signed more autographs, and left. The conversation about the letter to the Board resumed. "I think we'll get some action," a parent said. "Ever since that picketing we did in 1961, we can discuss things with them on a more or less equal level. At least *I* feel equal. I'm not so sure how the Board feels."

I noticed Shapiro leaving the room and joined him. "Having Davis here," he said, "was a good experience all around. He's absolutely right about that need for pride in your past." I had been wondering about Shapiro's own background and the development in him of the kind of self-confidence that made him so open to people of quite different histories.

VII

Elliott Shapiro was born in Washington Heights on March 15, 1911. His father, George, had come to America from a large city in Lithuania that was known then as Kovno and is now known as Kaunas. His mother, Lily, was from Vilna, the capital of Lithuania. They did not know each other in Europe, but both came to New York in 1893, met a few years after, and were married in 1903. They had three sons. Edwin, born in 1913, is now comfortably retired after a career as a dealer and expert in rare coins. David, born in 1919, is principal of P.S. 611 in Queens, and acting president of the association made up of all the principals of the 600 Schools, which handle children with emotional and behavioral problems. He has a Ph.D. in clinical psychology, and is a practicing psychologist—as is his brother Elliott.

Elliott Shapiro remembers his father with warmth and pride. "He was not a learned man, but he was very interested in ideas. The first books I remember in the house were the Harvard Classics. Also, unlike most European-born fathers, he would join us in sports. Since we were one of the very few Jewish families in Flatbush, a tough neighborhood at the time, my father taught me boxing so that I could handle myself." Shapiro developed into an unusually skilled boxer. When he was twenty-eight, in an exhibition bout, he outpointed a man who later became middleweight champion. "I won't give his name," says Shapiro, "because it would embarrass him.

"During those years in Flatbush, from the time I was three to about the age of eleven, I had to establish myself in the streets with my fists practically every day. I remember an elderly Jewish man with a caftan and a long white beard passing through the neighborhood one day. Some of the kids began to make fun of him—yelling, 'Fox in the bush.' I felt it was my responsibility to defend him. I dreaded that kind of responsibility, it was so gratuitous a burden. But somehow or other I felt I had to help him. And I did. Another time, when I was nine, I had a fight with a kid two years older than I, and a lot bigger. It was toward evening, near a subway exit, and we soon had about five hundred people of all ages watching us. I got the impression that all of them were on the other kid's side, me being Jewish. Suddenly my father came up the stairs, saw what was going on, and stopped the fight. He took off his belt and marched me home with a great show of indignation that a son of his had been brawling in the street. Once inside our house, he shook my hand in congratulation."

Gradually the neighborhood changed, but Shapiro remembers that a year after he started attending Erasmus Hall High School, a Jewish boy for the first time won the presidency of the General Organization—a student government body. As a result, Shapiro remembers, "for a while, many of the Gentile boys wore black armbands."

George Shapiro had started work in America in his brother's factory, which manufactured cast-iron stoves, moved into the shoe business in Flatbush, and then tried operating a jewelry store in Bath Beach. That business failed, and George Shapiro became a salesman to drugstores. While in elementary school, Elliott Shapiro had started delivering newspapers, and by the time he was sixteen, he had become branch manager of a morning newspaper delivery route. Through high school, he had also worked in a steam laundry and in a shoe factory. In 1927, his father died of pernicious anemia. His mother was to live until 1950.

On finishing high school in 1928, Shapiro had to continue working to help support the family. He was hired at the North American Ironworks, in 1929, as an errand boy, and the duties of junior draftsman and bookkeeper were soon added. His mother also worked for a time—selling shirts, socks, and underwear from house to house. "She worked against enormous odds to keep us together," Shapiro recalls, "and it may be that I've associated the many courageous Negro mothers I've known with my mother."

In 1930, as business declined sharply, Shapiro was laid off. He enrolled for day courses at the Maxwell Teachers Training College in Brooklyn. Nights and weekends he worked at a subway newsstand, but he found time to join the debating society, along with the boxing and baseball teams. He also captained the fencing team and won a college essay prize. He had chosen the theory of relativity as his subject because, he recalls, "I wanted to show that the theory *was* understandable to more than twelve men in the world, and I also wanted to give my interpretation of it."

Two years after he started classes at Maxwell Teachers College, the school closed, since there had been a precipitous drop in employment opportunities for teachers. Shapiro found jobs at a jewelry store and at a shop selling malt and hops. "I eventually discovered," he says, "that the store was a disguise for a bootlegging operation. One time I was carrying a big bronze object through the streets of Yorkville, innocent of the fact that it was a still. Policemen were looking at me, but I guess they figured anyone carrying a still in the open *had* to be innocent." While working, Shapiro enrolled for a year at the City College of New York and acquired enough credits for a New York State teaching license. The license did not permit him to be hired as part of the New York City public school system, but when a W.P.A. job in remedial reading opened at P.S. 202 in Brooklyn in 1935, he accepted it. At the school he soon became an active organizer for the teachers' union despite the principal's advice that he could go far in the school system—once he had passed the examination for a city teaching license—if he were to restrain his organizing fervor.

In 1936, Shapiro started to teach reading in the children's ward of the psychiatric division at Bellevue Hospital. Having taken the requisite examinations and obtained a New York City Board of Examiners teaching license in 1937, he moved to the adolescent ward in the psychiatric division of the hospital, and there he remained for eleven years. "They were mostly poor kids," says Shapiro. "At first the highest percentages were of Italian and Irish. By 1948 about half were Negro, and now some ninety per cent are Negro and Puerto Rican." The classes were small—from eight to twelve children to a teacher—and Shapiro's responsibilities included teaching English and arithmetic, although the heavy emphasis was on reading. During those years, Shapiro was an interested observer at the Bellevue psychiatric clinics. Adolph Woltmann, now teaching at C.C.N.Y., had developed a series of dramatic plays with hand puppets that allowed the children to identify with a wide range of situations. They were encouraged to shout advice to the puppets, and what the children said was written down for diagnostic discussion. Shapiro absorbed more about the dynamics of the learning process through the work in clay modeling conducted by Dr. Lauretta Bender and Mr. Woltmann. Increasingly he read in the field and participated in conferences at the hospital. "In eleven years," Shapiro estimates, "I must have attended almost fifteen hundred diagnostic sessions, and that gave me a pretty solid background."

Shapiro had meanwhile continued his academic education, achieving a Bachelor of Science degree in education at New York University in 1937. From 1939 to 1940, he studied social philosophy and psychology at the New School for Social Research, took four courses in history at Cornell during the summer of 1940, and the next summer studied social pathology and social problems at the University of New Hampshire. In 1946 he added a master's degree in guidance and school administration from New York University, and he received a Ph.D. in clinical psychology from the New York University School of Education in 1959.

Shapiro in 1948 had become the first principal of P.S. 612 in Brooklyn, which had just been set up in the psychiatric division of Kings County Hospital as one of the first of the 600 Schools organized for children with emotional and behavior problems. (When he started there, Shapiro had a teacher-in-charge license, and eventually passed the examinations for junior principal and senior principal licenses.)

Having begun with classes in a ward for patients, Shapiro in 1950 set up a day school at Kings County Hospital for children who otherwise would have been sent away to Rockland State, Creedmore, or other state institutions. The school, moreover, also became able to enroll some children who had already been institutionalized and were now permitted to return to their homes and attend classes at the hospital. The then superintendent of Kings County Hospital, no partisan of psychiatry, ordered the closing of the day school in 1952, on the ground that the space was needed for medical purposes. Despite Shapiro's complaint to the Board of Education, the superintendent's order was carried out. For many months, Shapiro continued to fight the closing, and finally the Commissioner of Hospitals ordered the reopening of the day school.

Although an appointment was offered to Shapiro at that time as a principal elsewhere in the school system, he turned it down, preferring to stay on for a year or two and protect the children in his day school from any further attempts to close it. Finally, in 1954, he did ask for another position and became principal of P.S. 119 in Harlem. "My first preference," he says, "had been a school in the Bedford-Stuyvesant area, because I was living near there at the time, but I'm glad the Board sent me to P.S. 119, because it soon became evident to me that the people in Harlem had a strong feeling for the place. That kind of spirit did not exist nearly so firmly in Bedford-Stuyvesant.

"I was looking for a challenging school," Shapiro continues, "because I had a fairly unusual background and felt I was qualified to deal with children who had problems. I came to Harlem, however, with some presuppositions that I found out were wrong. I had expected that children, growing up crowded together in broken homes, would present problems similar to those manifested by neurotic children. I have discovered that, on the whole, they do not. Most of the children here are as 'normal' as children in middle-class neighborhoods. But they do have overwhelming problems to deal with. It's to their credit that they maintain their courage as long as they do, especially when you consider that those of us who should be giving them support—teachers, school principals, and social service personnel in general—are unable to because we're so outnumbered. I found out that, for

the most part, I was not working with neurotic children but
with deprived children. And people like me were among those
who had been depriving them. It also became clear that my
work as principal had to extend into the community."

As Shapiro became immersed in the problems of the
parents as well as those of the children, he was, in a sense,
returning to a preoccupation of his earlier years. From 1931
to 1933, he had worked on the development of leagues of the
unemployed in Flatbush, and at one point he had accepted
an invitation to speak in Harlem on the techniques of organizing the leagues. He had given his talk at St. Philip's
Church, which was on the same block as P.S. 119. In 1937,
he participated in the Interracial March on Congress for
increased appropriation for social welfare. "It was probably," Shapiro says, "the first large-scale interracial march
since shortly after the Civil War. There were about ten
thousand of us. We camped overnight in the rain before the
march on the city itself. Some of us actually got into Congress, crowding the balcony of the House. From the floor,
several Congressmen spoke directly to us. The demonstration
resulted in a billion dollars more in appropriations, even
though before we came the odds had been very much against
Congress's voting additional funds. A further result was that
the national economy was demonstrably improved for a
year."

Twenty-six years later, Shapiro—this time with his wife
and two children—was in the capital for another interracial
demonstration—the 1963 March on Washington for Jobs and
Freedom. They had come by train with a delegation from
the Negro American Labor Council, but became separated
from them at the station. The Shapiro family found itself
marching under the banners—in Yiddish—of the Jewish
Socialist Bund. "Is this a good organization?" his puzzled
seventeen-year-old daughter asked him. Shapiro, who had

known the organization since the early thirties, answered, "It's one of the best."

As a young man, he had also engaged in civil liberties activities. In 1938, Shapiro was among a group that went to Jersey City to defend Norman Thomas's right to speak there. Thomas, splattered with eggs, was prevented from talking, and some of his entourage were arrested. "But," Shapiro adds, "we brought that case all the way to the Supreme Court, and our right to speak and demonstrate peacefully in the streets of Jersey City was upheld." During the next few years, Shapiro was active on the streets of Brooklyn, speaking and fighting for the right to hold public meetings countering the growing anti-Semitic movement in the city.

In 1944, he expended considerable time and energy in attempts to convince the labor movement that it should make itself heard in Washington on the development of peace aims that might significantly shorten the war. "What I suggested," he says, "was that our peace proposals include social welfare plans similar to the social security, unemployment insurance, and now Medicare programs of this country. I felt that if we could offer such plans to the people of what were going to be the occupied countries, they would have much more reason to pressure their governments to come to peace terms. I had been encouraged by the German response to the proposals in the early 1940s by William Beveridge, the British economist, for a full social security system for all citizens. Even though there was little evidence the German people had heard of the Beveridge program, their leadership was so concerned with its possible effect on the German populace that Goebbels and others spent a great deal of time on the radio trying to ridicule *that* kind of state planning." Shapiro distributed leaflets describing his plan within the labor movement, but they had little effect.

Our Children Are Dying

As the 1940s went on, Shapiro became somewhat less of an activist on issues outside of education. In addition to his teaching in the public school system, he was devoting more time to teaching in other contexts. He had started in 1940 to lecture in psychology to student nurses at Bellevue, continued his courses there until 1948, and, from that year until 1954, he was a lecturer at the Kings County Hospital School of Nursing. From 1948 to 1952, moreover, he lectured two to four nights a week at Brooklyn College on the psychology of the normal and the abnormal personality. Also on his teaching schedule from 1948 to 1955 were courses for the Board of Education's in-service program. There he lectured to teachers on the education of problem children.

Since 1961, Shapiro has been giving a course at the School of Education of C.C.N.Y. His classes are made up to a large extent of New York City public school teachers who are acquiring graduate credits. The course is titled, "Discipline and Behavior Problems," but Shapiro is quick to emphasize that he inherited the title. "What I actually try to do," he explains, "is to get the teachers to examine how complacent, presumptuous, and ignorant we are. I include myself. We look at the processes by which we ourselves drop out while remaining present in the classroom, and I indicate the possibilities teachers have for becoming really involved with the children and their problems—outside the classroom as well as inside." It is a popular course, and invariably, more students enroll than can be accepted. A further Shapiro academic affiliation since 1963 has been his participation in a Columbia University seminar on "The City." Experts from various disciplines, from outside as well as within the University, meet regularly to discuss urban problems.

Starting in 1951, Shapiro has also conducted a private practice as a psychologist. He works primarily as a psychotherapist rather than as a clinical psychologist. From 1950 to

1952, Shapiro was trained at the Institute for Gestalt Therapy in New York, where his analyst was Dr. Laura Perls, one of the founders of the Institute. He also studied and later worked there with Dr. Frederick Perls, Paul Goodman, and Dr. Paul Weisz. Shapiro taught at the Institute from 1952 to 1955 and again in 1959.

Shapiro's office hours at his home, in a large apartment building in Rego Park, Queens, begin at five in the afternoon on Mondays, Tuesdays, and Thursdays. "The time I give to psychotherapy," he feels, "prevents my being as good a principal as I could be, in that otherwise I would devote those hours to becoming more involved in the Harlem community. But with two children in college, my salary as a principal isn't enough. And my practice does give me insights I use as an educator that I might not otherwise have had."

About a third of Dr. Shapiro's practice used to consist of young children, but in recent years most of his patients have been young adults, including graduate students and some college faculty members. "I had to de-emphasize my work with the very young," Shapiro says, "because I was getting too old. You see, we would do many physical things together —boxing, wrestling, throwing basketballs, running around a schoolyard somewhere. Actually I feel I still could be that active physically, but I began to think I ought to be careful.

"There were a number of reasons why I believed—and still do believe—that physical activity can be vital in working with children. Certain kids are scared of physical activity, but by my involving myself in it too, their fears diminish. Also the styles in which the child plays can be very revealing. A third reason is that some children need a victory over a man, and there were times when I'd deliberately lose. And, depending on the game, it's possible to talk about many different kinds of things while you're playing. The subjects vary according to the game. For some youngsters, communication is easier that way than in the stationary doctor-patient relationship, because the talk isn't in the foreground."

When not teaching, studying, and practicing psychotherapy, Dr. Shapiro was also raising a family. In 1939, he married Florence Fishkin, a Phi Beta Kappa graduate of Hunter College, who had taught English and Latin in junior and senior high schools. Mrs. Shapiro continued to teach until 1944, shortly before their first child, George, was born. George has obtained his bachelor's degree *summa cum laude* in mathematics from Harvard, and is now working for his doctorate in the same subject. Their daughter, Ellen, is at Brandeis University, concentrating on fine arts and the history of art. With both children away from home, Mrs. Shapiro has resumed teaching Latin, part time, in the upper grades of the Ramaz School, a Hebrew school on East 82nd Street in Manhattan.

"Florence," says Shapiro, "has always been of enormous support. Whatever I was doing—from the fight to keep the day school open at Kings County Hospital to the furor over the rat at P.S. 119—she never cautioned me or expressed any fear that I might be jeopardizing my job. If she had, those periods of tension might have been more than I could have borne."

Mrs. Shapiro, moreover, takes considerable and sustained interest in her husband's work. She frequently visits P.S. 119, and in 1960, when there was a chance some of the girls in the school might meet the requirements for the junior high school operated by Hunter College, she helped tutor them. One was accepted—the first Harlem student to be taken at that school in many years. "When word came," Shapiro recalls, "a secretary came up to me in the hall. Her hands were shaking and she could hardly talk. Then *my* hands started to shake. A wave of exultant hysteria spread among the teachers. They laughed and cried, all at once. It was a testimony to the depth of those teachers' desire for their kids to make it. Even now, when I talk about it, I'm moved all over again."

VIII

When Shapiro took over as principal of P.S. 119 in 1954, morale was not notably high, partly because the school—teachers as well as children —was rigidly disciplined. One of the new principal's preoccupations during his first years in Harlem was the stabilization of the teaching staff by making P.S. 119 a school in which teachers felt free to experiment and in which they could depend on further support from an actively interested parent body which would fight along with them for more books and other materials for the children.

"In working with the teachers and the parents," Shapiro notes, "it took me a while to catch on to something that involved the basic nature of the way I was communicating with them. I mean some of the Negro teachers as well as some of the parents. Many Negroes—I'm not talking about the young militants in the civil rights movement—have become very sophisticated in dealing with the white man, in the sense of leading him to make decisions they want but in a way that allows the white man to believe it's *his* decision. One of the first times I caught this was in a conversation with a member of the custodial staff. I was nodding my head, agreeing and agreeing, and suddenly I found myself saying I would do something contrary to what I wanted to do. I'd been trapped. Then I realized this kind of thing had been happening often. And so I began turning that device around into a challenge. I'd say to the teachers, guidance counselors, and parents, 'Tell me what it is *you* want me to do.' We began to be in much more direct communication."

As Shapiro's candor and obvious commitment to the children drew more and more parents into support of the school, he also discovered how vital it was for him to become engaged in extracurricular problems. "It was very important to batter at the welfare agencies, to beat down the doors to get people accepted. I spent hours on the phone." During this early period, an assistant to the then Commissioner of Welfare, James Dumpson, said to Shapiro one day: "Considering all the time you spend with us, I don't see how you get much else done in that school. You seem to have departments of home welfare, housing, and community service at P.S. 119. Don't you have a department of education?"

Some of the other principals in Harlem have taken a dour view of Shapiro's activities outside the school. "You can't help but like Elliott," one of them has said, "but he bends so far backward that with him the Negro community, Negro teachers, Negro anything can do no wrong." In response to the conviction that a principal should be only an educator, Shapiro says, "I can rationalize what I do because if the child's life is catastrophic he can hardly be expected to learn. Of course, as a human being, I don't have to rationalize that part of my work at all."

Shapiro has been joined in his battles with the Welfare

Department and other social agencies by the school guidance
counselors; and when immediate crises occur, it is not uncom-
mon for Shapiro and members of the staff to give their own
money to prevent evictions or simply to provide food when
the Welfare Department is slow in processing an applica-
tion. They also often bring in clothing to distribute, and
several mornings I have seen the trunk of Shapiro's car
crammed with coats, sweaters, and other apparel.

On occasion Shapiro has tried to rehabilitate what he
terms "severely distressed" individuals in the neighborhood.
"One was a wino," Shapiro recalls. "I found out about him
because a nephew of his was in the school. We kept him
surviving, with his head not quite above water. Finally, the
Veterans' Administration stepped in and made his life bear-
able. That man never has realized his potential, but at least
he isn't dead."

"Watch Dr. Shapiro as he walks on the streets," says a
teacher at P.S. 119. "Some days it looks as if there isn't a
junkie in the neighborhood he doesn't know."

Shapiro has also tried increasingly to involve his teachers
in investigations of their pupils' living conditions and family
problems. Mrs. Florence Persons, a warm, alert former
teacher at P.S. 119 and now a District Guidance Coordinator
for District Six in upper Manhattan, remembers his enlisting
several staff members in the dilemmas of "a hard-core family
that was hard to reach and had almost every kind of problem
you could think of. He himself took on a drunken son in his
early twenties and gave him individual therapy once a week
for a year. And we followed up with each of that family's
children in the school, talking to them and trying to find out
the dynamics of what was going on at home. Then Shapiro
sent a science teacher to visit the home, ostensibly on an
errand of some kind. At a teachers' meeting, he was asked
to describe what he had seen. The teacher was near tears.

Because of that description and because of a number of well-planted questions by Shapiro, we decided as a staff to do something about this family and many others in similar straits. Along with the Parents' Association, we got involved in housing. We invited several experts on the subject to explain the rules and regulations, we helped people with particular problems, and we wrote a lot of letters to the authorities. Then, in 1962, when the City Planning Commission expressed interest in rehabilitating and redeveloping certain blocks, we went around the neighborhood with questionnaires so that we—and the Commission—would really know what the needs were. As a result, we convinced the Commission to extend its plans. Rehabilitation had originally been scheduled from 145th to 135th Streets, but they accepted our recommendation that the plan go down to 131st Street."

When the decision was made, moreover, to construct P.S. 119's replacement next door, Shapiro encouraged his teachers to find apartments for those about to be displaced by the new building and to check out the apartments recommended by the official relocation office. "He wanted us," says Mrs. Persons, "to see some of the hellholes people were being asked to move into, and he wanted us to get angry at what we saw. And we did. However, we never did go as far in housing as he wanted us to. It was just too big a problem. As for the relocation, for example, we did find some families a little better housing than had been offered them, but others moved into apartments that were at best mediocre. That happens with some of his projects. He'll go out on a limb, but other people can't always keep up with him. And it's also difficult to keep the neighborhood engaged in something that may not bring action until six months or a year from now. They need immediate results to keep them committed.

"There's only so much one man can do, even with the

kind of staff Shapiro has at 119. But sometimes you can see a net gain. Take that problem family he got us involved with. The oldest of the boys in the school had hardened by the time he was in the fourth grade. Shapiro, however, was able to reach him. And I worked with the middle brother and the girl in the first grade. Finally the mother found a place in the Bronx and moved the family there on her own. I don't know how much help we were, but I doubt if she would have been able to make that move without the initial impetus that came from us. She was a woman whose husband would beat her up periodically, disappear, and then return and beat her up again. But eventually she did muster the confidence to decide to get out. We kept the oldest of her younger children for a while, because he just didn't want to leave. Shapiro worked out a program for him that allowed him to visit me or any other teacher to whom he was close any time he felt a strain. He could just walk out of his class. It was an embryonic version of what Shapiro later allowed John to do. The boy traveled here from the Bronx every day, and we let him move at his own pace until he got stronger and was able to deal with more structured situations."

In addition to involving himself and his staff in neighborhood conditions, Shapiro has also—particularly within the past five years—been concerned with emphasizing American Negro and African history and culture in the curriculum. Three years ago, with Shapiro's encouragement, thirty-five of the staff, under the direction of Miss Beryle Banfield, now an assistant principal at P.S. 175 on 134th Street in Manhattan, prepared a manual for teachers on ways of introducing African material into elementary school classwork.

The seventy-five-page manual includes sections on African folklore, family life, games, music, dances, art, foods, and history along with a bibliography for teachers and another for children. In the preface, Shapiro wrote:

The history of Africa's earlier civilizations has been virtually omitted from textbooks and curricula of schools of every level, from elementary to college, everywhere in the world.

In a real sense, this hiatus, this long silence, has been a stilling of the voice of conscience. The fact that a strong and glorious voice was stilled is a measure of the avarice of those who profited from the canard that Africa has no history.

Now, at last, this long silence is coming to an end. Let us hope that our newly found ability to hear the voice of early Africa indicates that we now possess the will to live in the universal brotherhood that is absolutely essential for our survival.

The material presented in the following pages is a breaking of that silence. More and greater voices will be heard as early Africa receives its due, but it is to the everlasting credit of Miss Beryle Banfield and the committees of teachers who worked so devotedly with her that the first voice to be heard in any educational system anywhere was theirs.

Truly, they have been the pioneers, for we have been in the wilderness.

Requests for the manual have come from public school systems, church groups, social agencies, colleges, and individuals throughout the country. In the summer of 1964, sixty copies were in use in Mississippi Freedom Schools. There was also a demand for the manuals from the neighborhood. "People would come in off the street," Shapiro recalls, "and ask, 'Where is our history?'"

The one place from which interest in wider distribution of the guide did not come was the Board of Education. Copies had been sent to each of its members and to supervisory personnel. For a long time there was no response at all. Finally, two polite notes—but no offers to make the manual available throughout the school system—came from a member of the Board and from an assistant superintendent in charge of integration. The cost of preparing the manual had been borne entirely by the staff of P.S. 119, and much of its distribution was financed through a church group to which Mrs. Arthur Lanckton, a volunteer teacher at P.S. 119, belongs.

On the cover of the guide is a quotation from Edmund Burke: "A people will never look forward to posterity who never look backward to their ancestors." Shapiro has continued to operate on that conviction. In addition to classroom work on the Negro past, there have been African days and nights at the school. In 1964, for instance, some sixty of the children were trained in African dance by a professional African dancer. They performed at P.S. 119 before an overflow audience that included guests from African missions to the United Nations. Later the P.S. 119 dancers brought African culture to City Hall. For the event at the school, P.S. 119 parents prepared African food. "Our guests from the U.N.," Shapiro notes with pride, "certified that they were indeed African dishes."

"He obviously is fully committed to the concept of giving the children and their parents a strong sense of their past," says Mrs. Persons, who had been a guidance counselor at the school while the manual of African studies was being prepared. "But, as is often the case with Shapiro, more than one motive was involved in the first surge of interest in getting the guide together. Several years ago, about two-thirds of the Negroes on the staff became deeply involved with the African independence movement. They took courses in it, and all of a sudden, they recognized that they had a heritage and began to react. They reacted to the only white people they saw on a day-to-day basis—the white teachers at P.S. 119. There was clear and growing hostility between black and white, and it tore Shapiro apart. At one teachers' meeting, he tried—gently—to get them to recognize that they were all there together for the single goal of teaching the kids. But that went over their heads, so he determined to have everyone join that rise of pride in race. And that was one of the reasons he encouraged the compilation of the manual. Working on it united the school, and by the time everybody—black and white—had gotten saturated with Africa—the animosity had cooled off, as he had known it would. He is that hip."

I asked Mrs. Persons what her own initial impression of Shapiro had been. "P.S. 119 was my first teaching job," she said. "Nine years ago a friend of mine and I had just gotten our licenses and we went looking for a school we would want to teach in. At P.S. 119, while waiting for an interview with Dr. Shapiro, we watched him. We watched the courtesy and respect with which he talked to the parents. It's a respect all parents are entitled to, but poor parents don't often get it. Then there was his interview with us. He doesn't conduct exhaustive interviews. He acts according to his own sensitivities about human nature. And we were hired. At first I felt that here was the father I'd always hoped for. All-perfect, kind, good. I wanted to produce more and more to please Dad more. For most of my first year he never came into my room to observe a lesson. But he knew what was going on. The door would be open, and as he'd pass by, he'd hear what was being said—my tone of voice, the responses of the children. And he'd watch the number of parents who came in to see me, and later he'd talk to them. Finally, at the end of the term, he walked in, looked into the back closet, winked at me, and walked out. I guess that was his 'official' observation of the class.

"He's sensitive to many small things. He can tell what *your* problems and strengths are, and therefore, when you go to see him about some difficulty in class, he watches how *you* see the problem, whether you have an understanding of all the factors involved. And although he's always telling you about the good things you're doing, he'll often add a sentence. If you just keep basking in the compliments, you may not pick it up, but if you do, you'll realize later that he's prodded you into looking at a problem from another angle, into seeing it in another dimension.

"After I'd been in the school a couple of years, he suggested I try being a guidance counselor. I hadn't had any preparation for giving advice to other people—students, parents, and also other teachers—and I didn't think I knew enough. 'People try it,' he said. 'Work with the teachers. Let them feel free to come in and talk with you.'

"Well, little by little they did start coming, and from time to time, I'd talk to him about the problems I was working with. I learned to listen for the suggestions hidden inside his compliments, and gradually I began to feel I knew what I was doing. His style doesn't work with everyone. Some teachers don't pick up on his suggestions. And some become so used to his paternal way of giving that when he's a little tired and can't give to the same degree as he usually does, they become annoyed and itchy. Those are times when he should be more authoritative than he is. And he's not a saint. If a teacher has a raspy, irritating voice and a manner to match, he's likely to stay away from her for a while. There *is* a limit to how much he can give to everyone.

"Some days," Mrs. Persons smiled, "he's away from everybody. I used to call them 'gray days.' His gray eyes and gray hair and gray suit all seemed to be of a piece. On those days he'd be up on Cloud 9, sorting out 'values' and 'truth' and altogether being so intellectual that he'd lost us. But later, gradually, the results of that kind of thinking would come out in concrete form. Like his decision on how to cope with that period of black-and-white hostility among the staff. I still come to him for advice. Like once, I told him my present job was getting to be overwhelming at times. I have to work with our counselors, help set up guidance programs in several schools and for open enrollment. I'm also involved in preparing Negro children and their parents for adjustment to the white schools. I'd been getting a lot of calls at night. Everyone was looking to me to solve his problems. I was beginning to feel like a goddess, but one without divine powers. So I said to him, 'You get four times the amount of requests for advice that I do. How do you handle it?' 'Well,' he said, 'if you're just halfway honest—not solid honest, I'm not solid honest—people recognize that and want to hang on for dear life. But I have no halo. If I did, it would be on crooked. So I give what I can until I'm tired and can't give any more.'"

IX

One morning toward the end of the school year, I came to P.S. 119 and found Dr. Shapiro in what appeared to be one of his "gray days." He was abstracted, and looked tired. "There's a lot of Eichmann in everybody," he said without preliminaries. "I'm not talking about overt viciousness. I mean the strong tendency to go along, to conform. Look, while I've been principal of P.S. 119, in any given year more children are *not* educated than *are* educated. What do I do? Picket my school? Or do I pick those moments when I can do something effective about changing the situation? But there's always the possibility of corruption. As we let time go on, we ourselves develop a vested interest in keeping our mouths shut. We say to ourselves, This isn't the proper time. But any time will be difficult. What it amounts to is to try to keep yourself as conscious as possible of your basic assumptions so that you don't, in some unconscious way, move in a direction that alienates you from yourself and your hopes without your knowing it. The real problem is that we're finite. You can only do one thing at a time. And whatever you decide to do means that you've lost a chance to do something else. The danger is that you can always justify or rationalize those losses. I try to keep aware of the losses, and it's wearying. When I look depressed or tired it's because my consciousness of those losses is particularly close to the surface. My consciousness too of my inadequacy. There's so little you can do. But I don't blame myself. I recognize I'm doing as well as a human being can, and that's about it."

Shapiro stared out the window. "When you do decide to do something"—he seemed to be speaking more to himself than to me—"you have to undertake it with some reason to believe it can succeed. And that may require working hard to build a foundation for its success in various ways and through various channels that don't appear to be connected with what you want to do."

I asked him if there had been any new developments with Duncan, the boy from whom he'd taken a knife earlier in the year. "We did have a kind of breakthrough the other day," Shapiro said, returning to specifics. "He came in and said a girl was bothering him. We intervened rapidly. It turned out he had been bothering the girl more than she had him, but she wasn't entirely blameless. And we made much of that. To Duncan, not to the girl. We talked to them separately.

"But"—Shapiro leaned back and closed his eyes for a moment—"I don't know if there's anything we can basically do with him for the short time he has left here. How do you pinpoint his problem? On the one hand, he's in a home without a man, and his mother beats the children more severely than most of our parents do. But then there's that possibility of his having an aphasic problem. That would mean he simply cannot reason abstractly. Maybe he's not testing us at all. Maybe he simply isn't getting what we're trying to tell him. Also he has tested as retarded, but he doesn't seem retarded to me. So where's the block?"

I asked about John. "We've been paying a lot of attention to a little first-grader who has some severe problems, and John is getting jealous. He picks on the boy verbally and physically. Yesterday John hit him in front of a lot of first-graders and kindergarten children. I had to separate them. John was sore and started swinging at me. I decided to let him. He took off his raincoat and swung so hard that he fell down. That was to show he meant business. Then he tore a picture off the wall—also to show he meant business. I walked away and he followed me. I told him, 'You're acting like a little boy, too. You're jealous of him.' 'I'll show you how much of a little boy I am,' he said, and took a real whack at me.

"Later he told a teacher he was sorry and was going to apologize. He came back to the office and started to work. Not a word from him. At lunchtime I couldn't go out and mentioned to one of the office workers that I had no coffee. A few minutes later I felt a hard sock on my back. It was John. 'Here's your coffee,' he said. It was the hardest sock he'd ever given me. Then I found out he's been going to class more than usual, and most lunchtimes he's been talking with Mrs. Lanckton about his reading and lots of other things. I think there's some real improvement there."

Leaving Dr. Shapiro in his office, I started to walk to Mr. Stephenson's fifth-grade class. On the way, I met Mrs. Lanckton. A tall, gentle woman in her fifties, Mrs. Lanckton told me that John had been coming to see her more and more often during the past two months, and not only in school. He often had dinner at her house in the East Seventies, had spent his birthday with her and her husband, and had been with them for a weekend at their place in Connecticut.

"At first," she said, "he would talk about how furious he was at the death of the woman who'd been taking care of him. He was convinced, he said, that the white doctor had purposely caused her death because he wanted to use her organs and cells. And he'd talk about Harlem being what it is because whites hate blacks. And about how he hated where he lived and how poor he was. Then he'd go into what he was reading and what he'd like to read. One day he said he was interested in civil engineering, and I got an engineer friend to send him a lot of material. When I gave it to him, John said he didn't care about engineering any longer. But when he thought no one was looking, he read it all very carefully."

Mrs. Lanckton went on to a small office space she shared with the lunchroom aides. Mr. Stephenson's class was visibly busy. One group of children was at a reading table, another at an arithmetic table, and others were writing compositions. The walls were crowded. On the bulletin board in the front of the room were columns by Roy Wilkins; a newspaper article on Mrs. Charlotte Moton Hubbard, a Deputy Assistant Secretary of State and a Negro; and a picture of the Selma-to-Montgomery March.

At the far side of the room was a bookcase with a sign, RESEARCH CENTER, over it. On the wall alongside were maps of the solar system and three batches of clippings headed INTERNATIONAL NEWS, CURRENT EVENTS, NATIONAL NEWS. "My goal with these children," said Stephenson vigorously, "is to develop basic skills and then get them into self-propelled, independent learning. These children are automatically trained for failure. We've got to break that lockstep. One way too many of the public schools entrench that training is by automatically promoting those who don't know anything.

That way we create sociopaths, and sometimes criminals. That kind of child never faces a problem, figuring he'll always get by. We have to train these children to make it, to learn how to take tests, for example. Since they're used to failing tests, they have a phobia about them. Also they have bad work habits. They don't know how to follow directions, how to listen. And that, too, affects their test performances. They're capable of more than the tests show, but they're used to turning you off."

There was a buzz of conversation from the far end of the room. "Excuse me," said Stephenson, raising his voice. "What," he asked the class, "is Rule One?"

"Respect for others, work quietly, and help, not hurt, each other," the children answered in chorus.

"Thank you," he said.

"What I'm after"—Stephenson pointed to the children writing compositions—"is verbal fluency. At this point I'm not concerned about whether the spelling is correct. They're not used to expressing themselves in words, and that comes before spelling. Rebecca," he said to a thin girl with pigtails at the reading table, "if you want to work, you'll have to work quietly." "She is either retarded," Stephenson whispered, "or has brain damage."

On the wall above a blackboard at the front of the room were various mottoes. HONOR IS PURCHASED BY THE GOOD DEEDS WE DO. RECIPE FOR SUCCESS: BEING PREPARED, PROPER WORK TOOLS, BEING UNSELFISH. "Mr. Wilson"—Stephenson was addressing a large, bulky boy at a table that had suddenly become noisy—"you're tablemaster of your table. So you're responsible for your group.

"It used to be," Stephenson said, turning to me, "that the child of whatever background was converted into an American by the public school system. Part of his culture became part of American culture, and he absorbed the majority culture.

Then he could make it in an integrated society. Furthermore, the child's peer group would let him integrate. But it no longer works that way. These children, because of their background, are at a considerable distance from the majority culture. And not enough effort is being taken to bring them in. Our system of public welfare has been one of the ways we destroy their potential and that of their parents to build a bridge to the larger society. I visit the homes and I've seen families that come here from the South with a different culture, a different—matriarchal—family structure, and few resources. Instead of training them to function in this society, the social agencies operate on the implicit assumption that they'll fail. They put them on the dole and keep them submerged. This reinforces the expectation of those with an ex-slave mentality that they'll always be at the bottom of the heap.

"One thing the school has to do," Stephenson continued, "is to take the learning styles of some of these children into account. Some learn physically, through motion. Some can learn complicated things through song and dance. Each culture can teach in different ways, to different tunes. And I also try to provide them with basic tools. Each child has an atlas, so he'll get a perspective on where the world is and where he is. Each has an abacus. Above all, I keep them interested. We work with programed instruction, with Cuisenaire Rods in math. We've built—or rather, they've built—an analogue computer. And I've changed the tradition that little work is to be expected in the classroom after Easter. Here they work until the very end of the school year. The thing is I expect a great deal of them. I make them *strain* so that they can experience success, and that success experience makes them work harder. Once the child gets that satisfaction, he'll work no matter what's happening at home." He pointed to one of the girls at the reading table. "She was reading on the second-grade level at the start of the year. Now she can read any of the fifth-grade books."

The hum of conversation in the room had grown louder. Stephenson turned to the class. "Listen position!" he announced firmly, and began what was obviously a ritual. He would start a sentence and leave the last word for the class to fill in.

"I'm not a—"

"Jailer."

"I refuse to be a—"

"Baby-sitter."

"I'm a—"

"Teacher."

"You are a—"

"Student."

"Your parents send you to school to—"

"Learn."

"They don't send you to school to—"

"Play and waste time."

"Thank you very much."

The ritual over, the children, silent, went back to work. "These children," said Stephenson, "are taught that being in this class is a privilege. They can't sit here unless they function in a certain way. I will remove a very unruly child. Destroying yourself is one thing. Destroying the others is something else."

Stephenson went back to his desk and a continuous stream of children went to him, turning in work, asking him to check their papers, and taking new assignments. During a pause he said, "Things weren't this efficient at the start of the year. For one thing, there's a lot of infantilism which, in a way, is encouraged by the school. Out of the children here, including some of those who just came up with their work, there were seven confirmed thumb-suckers last fall. I use one tech-

nique or another until I break them of it. One way is treating
the thumb-suckers as babies. That's effective, too, with other
problems. Take stealing. If someone in the family steals, you
just can't say stealing is wrong and expect to have it stick.
But if you say that a baby steals, that a baby can't control his
impulses, you make an impact. They get the idea that doing
something like that is being a baby. I move them into *positive*
activity. See those tables there near the Research Center. The
children set them up and refinished them. I have them do that
kind of work to develop the feeling that there are many different kinds of things they can accomplish, and that they can
make use of their energy constructively.

"It's more than a full-time job. I have a curriculum center
in my home that I use to prepare for the work here. I've set
up an after-school tutorial corps for some of them in conjunction with HARYOU-ACT; an after-school sports program at
the Y.M.C.A.; and I've organized a cadet corps, in an attempt
to build a positive gang approach. Also I'm a licensed guidance counselor.

"One thing I've learned above all is that we have to create
a feeling among these children of pupil *permission* to learn,
a feeling that the peer group allows constructive activity, including learning. And for that I have to create a strong and
firm atmosphere. These children live in fear. See that boy
with the patch on his head. There's a sadistic kid in the
school that hit him on the head with a rock last week. And
they fear change as well as violence. When they experience
change at home, it's something negative, whereas with other
kids, change is a positive experience. Along with the fears
is a poor self-image. What I have to do is create a climate
strong enough so that they'll feel free to learn, to experience.
And that way I can also build the confidence among these
children that they're *permitted* to learn by their peer group.
If I can get them *all* involved and interested, that confidence

can come into being. The hardest thing to give them is a feeling of security. That's why Mrs. Taylor, in that sense, is the best teacher we have. We give her the kids we can't handle."

I asked Stephenson about John, whom I had seen wandering along the corridors as I went to Stephenson's classroom. "I tried working with him, but I didn't realize how disturbed he was. I don't agree with the theory of just giving him a warm atmosphere and no other limits. A child needs limits in order to be able to define himself. Some of these kids don't know who they are. That's what I mean about breeding sociopaths. Alone, they'll never bother you. Together, they might kill you. They've got to learn inner control from outer control. As for John, they've allowed him to be an *idiot savant* around here. They haven't taught him to inhibit his aggressive instincts and they haven't helped him define himself. They tolerate him because he's the best reader in the school. O.K., he has no mother or father, but I have kids in my class in the same situation, and they achieve very well. The point is not to feel sorry for him. The point is to teach him and carry on regardless. If a child is allowed to act out his aggressive impulses, he gets worse. Like, some of the kids who've been in 600 Schools because they were disrupting classes in regular schools did well in that sort of strongly structured setting. But when they went back to a more permissive atmosphere, they started acting out again. This school has not helped John. It has reinforced his negative impulses, his negative energy."

The compositions had been turned in and I read through some as Stephenson walked to the arithmetic table to work with a puzzled student. One of the subjects assigned by Stephenson had been "If I Was Boss on My Block." One boy had written:

> If I was boss on my block nobody will mess with me. I will punish the person who mess with my mother. I will hit the person in the nose who mess with my friends.

A girl, if she ran her block, would:

make those bums and dope pushers to go somewhere else. Then I would tell the super to keep all the halls clean and the floor swept and moped and I would tell the kids around my block to put paper and wrappers in the can and keep the street neat and clean.

Another boy had decided:

If I was boss on my block I would beat up every body and take all of there money and buy me some ice cream and cup cake and I would eat it all and wouldn't give nobody any of it.

But a classmate had a different perspective:

If I was boss on my block I would take all the money that I could find and buy some reading books for all the children to read and learn. I would make the people stop acking so stupid. I would pick out sertin people to help me because even though I could be boss of the block, I could not do it all by myself. But right now knowbody is boss of the block and probly there never will be because in the project knowbody would take over. All they do is laught at everythin but that is the only good thing about them that everybody is friendly.

Another set of compositions was based on the theme, "Nobody Knows But Me." One girl had written:

Nobody but me knows that when I was small I saw my mother and she was really there. I did not tell no body but I was small at the time. I may sound crazy but it is the true. It was when we had a party and after that I never seen her again. But I know she is deid and I am so sorry for her.

"We read children's classics." Stephenson was back. "Like *Swiss Family Robinson*. I make it a family project. I let the children take the book home, they read it at home, we discuss it, and eventually many of them read it along with their parents. I have excellent cooperation from my parents. I make out, for instance, a printed homework schedule every week that has to be taken to the parents. They, in turn, check the homework and sign it if it's neat and complete. Some of the kids used to lie and say they didn't have any homework, but that's not possible now.

"These parents want their children to get the basic fundamentals. They want the children to *read*. And they want to make sure the children are protected. They, too, live in fear because of the conditions in the neighborhood. And they know their children are quite aware of which building has the neighborhood pusher and which one has the numbers collector. So they want the child disciplined. Some will come in and say, 'Give him a whack with the ruler if he needs it.' Moreover, if the teacher shows the parents he *wants* them to help, many will make an extra effort. If a parent is good in penmanship, he or she helps the child in writing. Others have their children read to them. One mother is very excited because her child is reading her the Bible, and another has her kid read her the *Daily News*.

"Parents have helped here in the classroom, too. Parents supplied the varnish, the paintbrushes, and the sandpaper for those tables we fixed up. And I've brought mothers in as assistants to whom the children can read and say their tables. Other parents have taught little things they know about the Negro heritage. When we have the parents here and helping, that's the *complete* joining of the parent and the school.

"I want you to see something positive that's going on in the gym," said Stephenson. He walked to the door, opened it, and there was John on the floor of the corridor. Standing over him and laughing were two girls. "I'm gonna punch you in your goddamn mouth!" John yelled. He got up and chased the girls. "See what I mean," said Stephenson. "If you don't intervene and tell them certain kinds of behavior are not allowed, this is what happens. Oh, well, we'll be reading about John on the front pages one day."

Stephenson locked the door of the classroom, and we went into the gym. As usual, the room appeared to be in chaos—children running, shouting, throwing balls, laughing, roaring. In one corner, however, a chunky boy of ten or eleven was leading five other youngsters in a set of military drill patterns. "That leader," Stephenson noted with satisfaction, "used to constantly hit girls. I had to carry him downstairs to the principal's office a few times. Now he and his cadet corps are the best disciplined children in the gym. Next we're going to get them uniforms and keep the cadet corps going all year round."

X

Stephenson went back to his class-room. I remained in the gym, watching the multiple explosions of energy. In about ten minutes, the gym had been cleared except for a kindergarten class scurrying around Lawrence Greenfield, a teacher in his early thirties, whom Dr. Shapiro had pointed out to me before as the man who had been in charge, for two years, of the special second-grade class for emotionally disturbed children.

I walked over and introduced myself. "I'm giving them some extra time down here," he said, gesturing at the children. "The room gets too confining for them." A tiny girl, tears in her eyes, pulled at his pants. He knelt down, hugged her, listened to her, hugged her again, and she ambled away. I noticed on a bulletin board on the wall that Mrs. Bonnie Taylor was scheduled for four afternoons of choral singing, games, crafts, dancing, and drawing in the after-school program.

Suddenly John whizzed through the gym and out the door. I saw Harry Weber, the assistant principal for the upper three grades, looking after him, and I went over. Weber, a kindly, witty man with considerable admiration for Dr. Shapiro, is credited by the principal for being of great aid to him through his administrative skills and his concern for the children. Weber was frowning. "That boy is the basis of my only disagreement with Elliott. John emasculates the staff. Any teacher is conditioned to do something about a child who's acting up. But here the teachers have been conditioned to give John a lot of leeway. I just don't think you can let a neurotic boy loose in a school."

Weber left the gym, and I returned to Greenfield. I asked him about John. "I'm with Shapiro," Greenfield said. "There's merit to the arguments of those on the staff who want him controlled, but I'm for saving individuals short of endangering anyone else's life or limb. And John hasn't really done that. Maybe Dr. Shapiro is biased in his favor because John is so intelligent, but I guess I'd be biased in the same direction. I admire him for taking a chance with John, and I think he's winning. More discipline is, in one sense, the easy way. But if you were to clamp down on someone like John, he could explode and perhaps kill."

I asked Greenfield about Mr. Stephenson's conviction that the children in P.S. 119 needed firm, structured classroom situations so that they'd be equipped to get along in the outside world. "I admire Stephenson's dedication," Greenfield answered, "but I feel that in the lower grades so much can be lost in the anxiety of trying to take care of the child's intellect. It seems to me we have to build basic human strengths here, and where else but in an elementary school ought you to work on giving children the confidence to get a sense of themselves? Hopefully, in that kind of classroom, the child will develop enough autonomy and emotional strength so that when he's ready to move academically, he'll move fast. You know, at A. S. Neill's Summerhill, there are children who don't decide until they're thirteen or fourteen that they want to achieve academically, but then, because they have acquired basic human strengths through the Summerhill experience, they make up four to six years of work in two years.

"Let me give you an example," Greenfield said, keeping an eye on the racing children, "of what often has to be done first in this school before we start worrying too much about academic achievement. Last year I taught a third-grade class. One of the girls was very bright, very perceptive, and yet her academic record was low. She was the kind of child most teachers would describe as a nice kid but without any particularly sparkling potential. For her first two years here she'd had good teachers of the academic kind. They concentrated on getting in the fundamentals. And there she was, projecting such tremendous anxiety that it was heart-rending to watch her. Her attention span, moreover, was minuscule. I figured the hell with her achievement, this kid needs something from *me*. For two months, if she wanted to read, fine; if she didn't want to read, that was all right too. When she became tense, I'd let her stop what she was doing, come to me, and put her head in my lap. And I let her feel able to cry. I can usually sense in a failure situation when a child wants to cry, but many are afraid of that kind of relief. So you have to make the first move, in a way that lets them accept your invitation to get it out if they're able to at the time. And they also have to be free not to accept it. If you're open, sooner or later, most of them will come to you. The tears will burst out in a gush of anxiety. And the process of contact and resolution goes on as long as the child needs it. Well, that girl, by the end of the year, had achieved a great deal academically. I see her around now and she's a much calmer, healthier, and happier girl. Sure, I have qualms occasionally in working with children like her that the breakthrough won't be made, but this child did grow—first emotionally and then in her work. With some children close contact—comforting them—is essential to starting the learning process."

It was time for Greenfield to take the children to the lunchroom. In a few minutes, he came back to the gym. "There are disappointments," he resumed. "When I had that second-grade class, there was a boy, Tommy, who was full of life and also maddeningly distracting. He couldn't concentrate for five consecutive seconds. After six months of complete frustration with him, I gave up. Although we had achieved rapport, Tommy was one of the few children who made just about no academic progress. For my own sake and that of the class, I put him by himself at a desk right in front of mine. I let him have clay, airplanes, and other things that captured his imagination and allowed him his private world without distracting the other children.

"I did this with a great sense of defeat. I'd tried everything I and my supervisors could think of. I'm still convinced that in a one-to-one situation—one teacher to him—or in a much smaller class, he could have progressed. Anyway, by doing that, I was able to pay more attention to the children who were more receptive, and I did see definite, concrete results with them. As for Tommy, for all the exasperation he caused, I couldn't help marvel at and admire the tenacious grip he maintained on his world. And his world was varied and interesting. He easily surpassed the other children in the class in worldly knowledge. He had a particularly exalted opinion of Cincinnati, where he had spent two summers with his cousin. To Tommy, Cincinnati was a synonym for heaven.

"One day in May, a girl had been absent for two days. I knew that the children were much swifter sources of information about each other than official channels, so I asked if anyone knew what was wrong with Sara. They told me she had moved. Actually, for the first time, they were wrong. She was back the next week. But we thought she was gone, and I said to the class that it was too bad she hadn't had a chance to say good-by. Tommy, playing with some toy soldiers at his desk, looked up, gave a good-by wave, and said plaintively, 'Bye-bye, Sara, see you in Cincinnati.' I broke up. Seeing me laughing, Tommy broke up too. He had summed up so much—the loss of a loved one without being able to tell her how much you regretted that loss, and the wish to be reunited in a beloved place. He'd done it so succinctly and so characteristically in his own language.

"At the end of the year with me, we had to hold him back. On the last day of school, Miss Jones, my supervisor, sent for him and broke the news. Earlier, among my techniques to try reaching Tommy, I'd mentioned the possibility he might be held back, but he hadn't paid any attention. The following fall, Tommy was tested at Bellevue and was sent to Rockland State. But before then, he'd visited my class regularly for the first few weeks of the new term. During one of those visits, I was trying to get my new class to understand the importance of listening, when Tommy suddenly asked if he could talk to the class about it. Those spontaneous interruptions of his usually broke my short-term plan of the moment, but I'd give him full rein, because the interruptions invariably enriched the life of the classroom. They were so starkly real. What I had just been saying apparently had corresponded to something in his world. He had tuned it in and reacted spontaneously. That means, by the way, that he must have monitored everything.

"Tommy said that if they didn't listen, they wouldn't learn, and next June Miss Jones would leave them back. That had happened to him, and they should learn from it. He added that Miss Jones had never warned him what might happen, and when she did tell him, it was too late to do anything about it. Then he said, 'If we don't watch out, life can hit us in a way that's very sad. So wake up and don't let that happen to you.' He said it with such feeling that I was filled with tears. That coming from an eight-year-old boy who is supposed to have a sub-normal I.Q., whatever that means. When I found out he'd been sent to Rockland State, I felt like saying, 'So long, Tommy, see you in Cincinnati.'

"And sometimes," Greenfield continued, "if there is something you can do, it's not enough. In that second grade one year, there was a bright-faced little girl of seven, Mandy. She would cock her head to either side at about a thirty-degree angle, and as she smiled, her whole face, especially her eyes, lit up. From the neck down she was a combination of sores and old, dirty, torn clothes—a most unattractive morsel. But from the neck up—a fount of life. She was bright, but she was so busy defending herself, so preoccupied with struggling to live, that she couldn't stop to listen. And worst of all for her, she couldn't afford to make a mistake, to be wrong, not ever. I tried to teach her that mistakes were permitted without loss of love or status. But it seemed as if I couldn't communicate with her. She was emotionally overloading every situation, precluding any chance of seeing anything with clarity. Nevertheless, the cumulative effect of an accepting environment—day by day—in the classroom had its impact. As she felt more secure, she could relax enough to listen, at least when other children were involved.

"Finally a breakthrough came. In March, about six months into the school year, I was going through a comparable situation with a girl named Lisa. She, too, had so much emotional investment in not making a mistake that she couldn't digest what I was saying. But Mandy, sitting there, not directly involved, could identify with Lisa and see herself in a similar situation with me. In the middle of something I was

saying to Lisa, Mandy said to me, 'Hey, Big Nose!' Her tone
told me that she was somehow expressing a positive aware-
ness of me. I stopped talking to Lisa momentarily, because
I thought the interruption important, looked into Mandy's
eyes, smiled, said, 'Hi,' and returned to Lisa.

"The next couple of days Mandy was unusually silent and
watchful of me. I knew something was going on but wasn't
sure what it could be. On the third day, as I was again speaking to Lisa, Mandy interrupted with, 'Hey, Stupid!' in a tone
I can only characterize as harshly forced. Contempt and
hostility were in her voice. It was clear that, having had her
warmth accepted even when it was obliquely expressed, she
was trying to find out how her hostility would be received.
I pretended to be angry and said in my best angry tone,
'Don't you *dare* call me Stupid. My name is Big Nose.' "
Mandy looked at me for a long time and somehow under-
stood. Her wild, contemptuous manner was not acceptable.
Direct expression of her anger and fear would be dealt with
in some other way. But her positive connection to me had
been firmly established. Had I said my name was Mr. Greenfield, insisting on respect for my authority, she would have
felt all her feelings were unacceptable, and a good opportunity for her to gain in self-understanding would have been
missed.

"From then until June, it was mostly gravy. Her behavior
improved markedly and her work leaped forward. It was an
amazing turnabout. But I was her teacher, not her father.
And in June it ended. I knew of no way to prevent the terrible impact of separation on Mandy. Two summers and a
year with another teacher have gone by. A good teacher, but
not one with a big nose. And the sweet side of Mandy—the
beautiful human being who had begun to emerge, the real
girl—has slowly receded. I suppose I should have been philo-
sophical and realistic about it. There was nothing more I

could have done. She wasn't my responsibility after she'd left my class. But I *don't* feel good about it. It's a lousy feeling to be so helpless in the face of reality."

Greenfield was silent. We looked at a group of boys playing basketball. "Last summer," he said, "I was driving by the school. I saw another girl I'd been able to help, but she too had taken the separation in June very hard. There she was on the sidewalk, with a lackluster expression. When she saw me, it was as if recognizing me were a blow. Her emotions had been that strongly aroused. And just as quickly, those emotions were withdrawn. I saw her face steel to immobility. She raised her hand in a small wave. I waved back helplessly and felt like burning down the whole city. That's the job." Greenfield waved at me and walked back to the lunchroom.

XI

Two mornings later, I looked in on the kindergarten class of Mrs. Marguerite Butler. Dr. Shapiro had told me John had taken to spending some of his time there occasionally. A calm, pleasant woman in her thirties, Mrs. Butler was collecting crayons from the children. John, in a black sweater and blue jeans, sat, surly, in a far corner, chewing gum. I nodded to him. There was no response. "It's one of his off days," said Mrs. Butler. "He's sort of belligerent this morning, and I'm trying to ignore him. On his good days, he plays records for the children and works with them building with blocks. They look up to him. And sometimes he treats them. Yesterday he brought an ice-cream cone to the child who had done best with the blocks. You know, John has asked me to buy a trumpet he's had his eye on in a pawnshop in the neighborhood. It'll cost sixty-seven dollars. I told him I would if he did a good job here and didn't act up. But I'm surprised he didn't ask Dr. Shapiro instead of me. He'd be surer of getting it. A number of the kids feel free to ask Dr. Shapiro for different things and usually he somehow works it out. He got one child a typewriter once."

John rose and began handing out crackers and cups of juice to the children—there were twenty-two of them—sitting at the low tables. A little boy yelled at a girl next to him, and John rapped him on the head with a drumstick. "I asked John this morning if he'd had breakfast," said Mrs. Butler, "and he didn't answer. I expect that's one of the things wrong with him today. I'd hoped *he'd* take some juice and cookies, but he's too proud. Quite a few of the little ones also come in without breakfast.

"Many of these children are quite bright," she continued, "but it takes time to release their potential. At the beginning of the year, several didn't know their own names. They answered to other children's names. Many had never heard a nursery rhyme. Parents working long hours aren't eager to talk about Little Bo Peep at night. Some didn't know how to use crayons, because they hadn't seen any before. Others didn't know how to hang up their coats. But once they're exposed to this whole new world of school, they soak it up like a sponge. Most of them. Occasionally, by the end of the year, you can tell which ones are going to be in trouble. You see five-year-olds already trying to play hooky. And some already tell lies. They take notes home, don't give them to their parents, but say they have. I tell them I don't like children who lie, because if they lie, they'll eventually steal."

It was rest time, and all the children but one had put their heads down on the tables. "Lay down," said John to the nonconformist, "or I'll smack you."

"A funny boy, John," said Mrs. Butler. "He came in this morning, saw my drawer was full of junk, and he cleaned it up. But then he sulked. Yesterday, I asked him if he'd like to come in at a definite time each day to read a story to the children, and he seemed very happy about the idea. We'll see."

I asked Mrs. Butler whether many of the parents of her pupils visited the school. "Quite a few this year. Some you never see. I don't believe in waiting until a child has problems to send for a parent. If a child is doing very well, I'll send a note home asking to see the parent. And I do some visiting in the homes, but there are parents who are not so particular about your seeing the real-life situation. No matter how poor they are, they do have pride."

John had put on his porkpie hat. Mrs. Butler looked hard at him across the room. "John, men don't wear hats indoors, do they?"

"No," said John. The hat stayed on.

"John, you can't help *them*"— she pointed to the children— "if you don't know what to do yourself." John pulled off the hat and began prowling around the tables where the children were resting. He raised his hand to hit a little boy who was whispering, but Mrs. Butler frowned and he walked by. "John," she said, "likes the idea of supervising and bossing, but he doesn't quite know how to do it. I'll have to talk to him again about leaving the discipline to me."

I left to visit another kindergarten class. A file of five- and six-year-old children was coming down from the third floor. One youngster stepped out of line, and a gnarled teacher, her face sour, pushed him back in. "You should be in *sub*kindergarten," she growled. "If you won't behave, you'll be suspended."

Another teacher, Mrs. Marion Jackson, tall, slender, in her mid-forties, was coping with a restless class. It was almost time for them to go home. I asked her if she often visited the children's homes. "Not as much as I'd like to. I want the parents to set the time. I don't just walk in. I'll suggest I visit, ask which

time is best for me to come, and if they don't pick up on it, I'll
drop it there. But it does help. You find out things you couldn't
at school. I had one little girl who cried easily and took a
long time to adjust to the group. She lived with a grandmother whom I never saw. Finally, I did visit the home and
found out the child was overprotected. In trying to make up
for the absence of the mother, the grandmother had given
her too much of everything—dolls, toys, and the like. And
so, coming from a home where she had everything without
asking, it was hard for her to compete with the other children."

The children grew noisier. "I'm not going to speak to you
any more," Mrs. Jackson told them. "I've talked very nicely
to you, and I think it went in one ear and out the other." A
gap-toothed boy grinned. "Well"—she looked at her watch—
"it's time. I think we all need a vacation." The children raced
for the cloakroom in the back of the room, slid open the
doors, and grabbed their coats. Mrs. Jackson walked them
down to the yard, where their mothers or older brothers and
sisters were waiting.

When she returned, she spoke of another former pupil.
"There was a little boy last year. It was obvious he came from
a home with practically nothing. In the winter he'd come in
with no underwear, shoes without laces, and no socks. He
was so dirty the other children said he couldn't sit next to
them. He was so terribly ashamed. One day he told me his
mother had said I could come to see her. Actually, as I
found out, she hadn't said anything of the kind. You can
imagine the frigid reception I got. I tried very hard to explain to her what the lack of cleanliness was doing to her
son, but she had three other little ones and said she had no
time to look after him. 'But he's still a baby,' I told her. 'You
can't expect him to get himself off to school in the morning.'

"It was a very overcrowded apartment," Mrs. Jackson went

on. "Three rooms with several adults plus grandparents. I didn't know which were relatives and which weren't. The visit opened my eyes to how alone he was. It wasn't so much that his mother didn't care, but rather that she didn't know how to handle all she had to do. Accordingly, she had convinced herself he could make it on his own. After the visit, I took even more of an interest in him. I'd ask him if he had breakfast, and usually he hadn't. I brought him some of my own youngster's old clothes. I didn't know how his mother would accept that, but apparently it was all right, because he wore them until they were practically unrecognizable. That boy tried so hard to please me. He always wanted my approval. I had to keep on reassuring him, because probably no one ever recognized him at home, let alone said he had done something good. He was bright, and worked as hard as he could, but this was the only place he got any encouragement. By the end of the year, he was getting along well with the group, but I don't know what happened to him after he left my class. Now if this school is right for him all the way through the sixth grade, that could make a difference. Imagine, that boy being pushed out on his own at five! My God, if he were ten, his mother would send him out to get a job. Dr. Shapiro tells us, 'When they want to cry, let them cry.' They don't have much chance to cry at home, and some have a lot to cry about.

"I wouldn't want to teach anywhere else but here," Mrs. Jackson said. "Because of Dr. Shapiro. My first year here I was walking with another teacher who'd been at P.S. 119 a while and we saw him come out of a house on Eighth Avenue that I wouldn't have had the courage to go into without a guard. If then. 'What on earth is he doing *there?*' I asked. 'Oh,' she said casually, 'he's looking for a child. He does it all the time.' I tell you he came stepping out of there as if he were coming out of his own house. That man will go any place and do anything." She laughed. "In one of the upper classes a few weeks ago, a boy was asked to give the names of the Great Lakes. He got through four of them and stopped. Finally he tried 'Lake Shapiro.' He figured Dr. Shapiro was a big enough man to have had at least a lake named after him."

On my way to Shapiro's office, another line of children came downstairs on the way to lunch. A thin, middle-aged teacher, harried, rasped, "Excuse me, would you like lunch or not? I think"—her voice rose sharply—"some of us are not ready for lunch. Get over by this wall!" she snapped at an eight-year-old. "And you." She turned to three whispering girls. "I'd like you to keep your mouths shut. All right, let's go. This is *not* second-grade behavior!"

As she marched down the stairs, behind her stood a girl in braids, her arms akimbo. She looked at the teacher's back not so much with hostility as with amused disdain. I noticed a new wall display in the second-floor corridor leading to the principal's office. It was a pictorial history of Ghana, and the text began: "Once upon a time, long before Columbus discovered America, there were great kingdoms in West Africa."

I told Shapiro about the two teachers who had sounded like turnkeys. He looked pained. "That's terrible. I know who they are. I've talked to them a number of times about yelling at the children. They've been doing better, but I'll have to talk to them again. Maybe they had a bad time with their husbands this morning. I feel very weary when I hear about things like that." Shapiro looked more weary when I mentioned that a kindergarten teacher had told her children that if they lied, they would eventually steal.

He sighed. "By this time," he said, "every one of those children has told a lie. Now they've been given permission to steal. In fact, they'll be disloyal to their teacher if they don't steal. But even if I were to indicate my displeasure with teachers who say this kind of thing, their lack of knowledge of group dynamics will come out in another way. What we really need are workshops in group dynamics and group therapy for the teachers, especially teachers of young children. I did teach such a workshop once for a year at the Institute of Gestalt Therapy. We had about ten in the class, private and public school teachers. Then I tried it at City College, but there were thirty-five in that class, and that was too many. Sometimes what comes to the surface can be very wounding and there isn't the chance to assuage the hurt before the period ends. We need small groups—no more than eight teachers—and the workshops should last from one to two years, under instructors who have had expert training in psychology.

"What we need and what we have," said Shapiro, "are so far apart. Do you know that up to this year—and I don't know that it's changed—the Bureau of Child Guidance provided positions for only six psychologists and six social workers for all the children in all grades north of 125th street? That's thirty thousand children. And not all of those positions are covered. Furthermore, two-thirds of the psychologists' work—by mandate—is involved with testing children for placement in classes for those with retarded mental development."

John's caseworker from the Bureau of Attendance came in to see Shapiro. The principal introduced him to me and then excused himself, as he saw a secretary beckoning to him from the outer office. A tall Negro with glasses and a deep voice, the caseworker began comparing Shapiro with the other principals in his experience. "Most of them," he said, "don't want to make any waves. Waves might mean trouble and put a blemish on their record with the Board. So their schools are little white ivory towers taking no responsibility for what's going on in the community. They're so damn insecure they actually try to isolate their schools from the community. Some principals are just plain afraid, and both the staff and the children sense the fear. In schools like that, the children are, to a great extent, in control. The reactions of the staff and the supervisory personnel are built around their fear of the children. I get around to some twenty-five schools in the Harlem area, and believe me, Dr. Shapiro is *very* unusual."

John peeked around the door. In his hand was a green-and-black gun. The caseworker grinned. "If that's loaded—" he said in mock menace.

"Go ahead," said John, "try it."

The caseworker put his finger in the nozzle, and a thin stream of water fizzled out. John laughed and went back to the Thermofax machine in the outer office.

"Don't underestimate," the caseworker turned to me, "what these kids *could* become. Sheltered kids exposed to what these children go through every day would have collapsed a long time ago. Some of the ones in trouble we catch in time. Some we don't, but they live reasonably O.K. lives, except they never realize their full potential. And some are doomed."

XII

I didn't see Dr. Shapiro and P.S. 119 again until early October. Walking to the school along 133rd Street one morning, I saw Shapiro come out the door. He motioned me to join him as he walked around the block to put a dime in the parking meter next to where he had left his car on 134th street. As we turned the corner, we noticed a police car. It was parked, and two patrolmen were sitting in it. "I'm concerned," Shapiro said. "Across the street from the school, on the other side of the building, there's an apartment to which a lot of teenage boys and girls have been gravitating a little before noon most days. I don't know what's going on. Maybe marijuana or other things. Now should I report it and thereby get the kids into real trouble with the police? Or do I do them more harm by not reporting it? Suppose whatever is going on leads to their taking up heroin? And why haven't the police found out? I did, just by keeping my eyes open. There are things the police deliberately don't notice. Like they let numbers runners operate. But is letting that happen bad? After all, the community wants it. Numbers are the poor man's stock exchange."

As we started to come back to P.S. 119 through the yard, a group of first-graders, roaring out for recess, rushed up to Shapiro. Several, grinning, yelled, "Daddy!" and others had complaints, stories, or just wanted to say hello. A teacher extricated him. "It wasn't so tumultuous today," he smiled, "as it's sometimes been. Last year, I was getting so mauled for a while that I finally stopped going through the yard for a month or so when they were there. After I resumed, the intensity of the reception was somewhat diminished."

The teacher rushed over to a corner to caution a youngster against running too fast. "I know we have to have restrictions here," Shapiro said, looking after her, "but I can't stand having too many of them. We set up rules for the yard, and I nibble away at them when I can. We must have the rules, but they interfere with the development of the children. The children should be lively, playful, physically active. To deprive them of the chance to be as active as they like is to deprive them of their rights. Ideally, we should have fewer children in the yard or a much larger yard."

On the stairs, Shapiro was stopped by Harry Weber. They conferred briefly, and Shapiro walked on. "There's a teacher who's been late again," Shapiro said to me. "In the course of a year, she may be late fifty times. But she has good qualities that compensate for that. I'm certainly not going to write her a strong note. That would hurt her morale. We'll talk privately, although I'm not optimistic we can change *that* character trait. If she *lived* in the school, she'd be late. It's a neurosis."

Shapiro began telling me about a trip he'd taken to the San Francisco area since I'd last seen him. He had been invited to lecture at the graduate internship program for teachers at the University of California at Berkeley. "I also looked into the public school situation there. Unfortunately the teachers' organizations are weak. So, when I had a chance to address a dinner meeting of the public school administrators of the Bay Area, I tried to show them that their schools would be much improved if they didn't try to inhibit the growth of a strong union. Look how particularly important that kind of support is, I said, for a teacher in a deprived neighborhood. People living in a ghetto, crowded as it is, are alone. That's why they need support. And a teacher alone in a classroom needs support. I also urged them not to use their power against lively, creative teaching just because those teaching styles might not be among the officially approved methods. Imaginative teaching is exactly what poor kids need.

"And having said that," Shapiro continued, "I told the administrators that if they were, nonetheless, too strict or too quick to retaliate against unorthodox teachers or union activity, the results would be on their consciences. Before I left," Shapiro smiled, "someone reported to me that a rather influential man had said, 'We must have Shapiro in this school system at any cost.' And that's the last I've heard about that."

For the new school year, it had been necessary for Shapiro to hire several new teachers, and when we were back in his office, I asked him what his criteria were. "Well, if I can see an applicant on the job first as a student teacher, I can perhaps tell something about her capacities, but I've made mistakes even then. One thing I look for is whether they have a feeling, a liking for children. And whether they have the ability to identify with the needs of the children and of the parents. Are they likely to become self-righteous and recriminatory about parents who, for various reasons, can't or won't come to school often? Then, when I locate a man, I'm apt to be biased in his favor because our children—and for that matter, children in all elementary schools—need more men teachers. Young children are mostly in contact with mothers or substitute mothers, but young girls and boys need to be able to relate to an adult male. Boys, obviously in order to get encouragement to develop ego models; and girls, so that they can more easily accept their essential feminine worth.

"One problem is you may find a teacher—male or female—who appears to have many excellent qualities, and yet that very teacher may do worse in her first year than mediocre colleagues. It's the class size. The best teachers are apt to be those most reluctant to set up routines—ways of passing out paper, raising a hand for recognition to speak or leave the room or go to the wardrobe. They're reluctant because they'd prefer a more human, spontaneous atmosphere in the classroom. But if the class is large, they have to develop routines because they're so outnumbered. They have to show they can control the class. And in the process, their humanity is attenuated. In order to survive, they have to go against their better nature. They're trapped, even as I'm trapped by having to permit more rules in the school than I'd like. And so, when classes are too large, even in the warmest teacher something is lost. As the years go on, moreover, if the classes *remain* large, more and more is lost."

I wondered what he thought of the teacher-training programs in the colleges. "They're not useless, and it's probably better to have them than not, but too often they're given by professors who have had very little experience in large urban school systems. They're not only, by and large, too theoretical, but they're unreal insofar as our kind of school is concerned. For one thing, the professors tend to develop methods and practices that pertain to middle-class suburban school systems, where the class sizes are small. Or, when purportedly dealing with the big city schools, professors often underrate the many poor children who attend those schools. At the same time, they overestimate the help young teachers receive when they break into the public school system. As a result, new teachers become quite discouraged when that degree of assistance isn't forthcoming.

"As for what should be emphasized, I don't like to see someone who's been entirely an education major. The teacher ought to have a major interest in at least one other subject—social studies or math or English—and a good liberal arts background, in general. Also, at one point or another—in the senior year or after graduation—the prospective teacher should become involved in an intensified internship program, much like a medical internship. I mean working in a public school and attending workshops held in that school. Workshops based on a critical evaluation of what they've participated in and perceived in the classrooms, the corridors, the schoolyards, and at parents' meetings. And there ought to be another workshop on how the teacher can become a citizen of the school and of the community.

"That," said Shapiro forcefully, "is why I'd especially like to see teacher-training programs oriented toward trade unionism. In New York City, the United Federation of Teachers is providing a structure of support so that the teacher *can* be lively, energetic, and inventive without fear of reprisals. Now 'lively' is a tricky word in some cases. I've said that our children are lively, and they are; but sometimes what seems to be liveliness may be a galvanic response after the rest of the body has been killed. It may be an irritability left over after the rest of the body has died. But let us grant the essential liveliness of our children. How does a teacher make the most of that liveliness, and how can he best avoid dampening it?

"Suppose, for example, in a social science lesson, the

teacher is talking about this being a democratic society. And a kid says, 'Teach, we have no heat at home. What do we do in this democratic society to get heat?' If the teacher doesn't formulate some plan in which the children can participate— picketing or other ways that might change the situation—the children won't buy the lesson. In New York, because of the U.F.T., teachers *can* work out that sort of plan. They can capitalize on the real liveliness in the children and they can extend irritability into liveliness. Almost nowhere else in the country can a teacher do this. But so far, hardly any New York teachers *know* the scope of the possibilities in this direction. They don't have a full enough sense of their own strength through the grievance machinery that's been set up.

"Previously, if a teacher in the system had advocated, let us say, a rent strike, the principal could forbid it. And most would have forbidden it on the ground that a rent strike is not proper activity for a teacher. If the teacher had gone ahead, he would have been found guilty of insubordination or of conduct unbecoming a teacher. So, under those circumstances, it was more than an existential act for a teacher to follow through. It was a reckless act. Now teachers *can* follow through, but the U.F.T. leadership is failing in its responsibility to make its members aware of the extent of this breakthrough.

"What I'm driving at is that when some educational theorists call for teachers to nurture the liveliness of slum kids, they must also recognize that once the liveliness *is* aroused, it cannot always be contained in a classroom. But since teachers outside New York City cannot go beyond the classroom, they'd be betraying the children in an example like the one I cited of *telling* them this is a democratic society but not showing them how to *make* it democratic for *them*. There would be no way for the children to *experience* that democracy in action. That's why, when I was asked recently at a meeting of educators whether I thought a teacher should first encourage the liveliness of his children or should first join the U.F.T., I said unhesitatingly that he should start by joining the U.F.T. Then, when he does nurture that liveliness—and is inevitably tested by the kids to take some kind of action inside the school or out—he's able to prove he's for real.

"You see, with this kind of protection from their union, teachers could be so important in advising, participating in, and stirring up community action. Not only about education, but about neighborhood rehabilitation and other problems that directly concern the children as well as their parents. Think of masses of teachers marching with parents and with other people in the community! That's an important new role for teachers to play—instead of being dropouts, as teachers and as human beings.

"An example," Shapiro continued, "of how a strong teachers' union can institute basic change in the school system itself has been the U.F.T.'s role in getting the 'More Effective Schools' plan adopted. Essentially, the plan was formulated by the union, although the plan the union advanced was initially rejected. It involves cutting class sizes in certain schools almost in half. I was a consultant with regard to class size, incidentally, and I recommended one adult to twelve children. If you remember, James Conant in *Slums and Suburbs* noted that in the wealthiest suburban areas, the adult-to-pupil ratio was one-to-fourteen. Twice the Board turned down —almost scornfully—the concept of reducing class sizes that drastically. They called the idea visionary, because, they said, there aren't enough teachers. We had to tell the Board that we're at the end of the teaching shortage. The first wave of World War II babies is moving into adulthood and many of them are becoming teachers. So it's inaccurate to keep planning on the basis of a lasting shortage of teachers.

"Anyway, a couple of years ago, Calvin Gross, the then Superintendent of Schools, asked that a plan for more effective schools really be formulated and considered. "Note"—Shapiro raised his eyebrows—"the term '*more* effective,' indicating that what had been going on had been at least 'effective.' Three groups of planners were set up—from headquarters, from supervisory personnel, and from the U.F.T. Only the U.F.T. came in with a cohesive plan, and that was the one adopted with some additions, compromises, and improvements. The U.F.T. plan, for example, provided that no More Effective School contain more than eight hundred pupils. The compromise was one thousand. But what did go through involved greatly increasing the number of teachers and specialists—and greatly reducing the class sizes—in the schools selected. In certain schools the size was cut in half. It marked the first time a city-wide educational plan had been largely stimulated by a teachers' union; and throughout the country, wherever there are U.F.T. locals, our plan is being used as a basis for drawing up local programs to be pressed on boards of education. It's the beginning of a vital trend which can make teachers' unions an active partner in developing educational policy."

The More Effective Schools program in New York City got a small start in ten elementary schools in September 1964, and ten more were added a year later. "I have my doubts," Shapiro said, "that all the principals whose schools were selected were right for the program. The Board's criterion appeared to be schools with enough classrooms, and it didn't sufficiently take into account all the principals' particular styles. But despite this drawback, the most recent test scores indicate that the plan is working to some extent. For the first time in recorded history here, so far is I know, children in slum neighborhoods are achieving one month's scheduled improvement—or better—for each month they're in class.

"We couldn't get P.S. 119 into the program because we didn't have enough classrooms, but I want our new school, P.S. 92, to be part of the plan. We *must* have it, because every month that goes by means more and more kids are crippled. So we have to move the community to demand it. Actually the community doesn't need that much moving. All we have to do is make the neighborhood aware that this opportunity can be opened for us. Knowing that, the parents won't need any prodding.

"As for the long run"—Shapiro looked grim—"I'm especially worried because, at this point, there seem to be some indications that the school system is rather cool to the expansion of the More Effective Schools program. Despite the clear, initial signs of success, there are strong forces within the system opposed to greatly increasing the number of More Effective Schools. My guess is those forces are worried about costs, forgetting in their anxiety about fiscal matters that children are worth everything we can give them. So *that* is going to have to be fought. Then there's another dimension to the plan that has not yet been fully accepted. In our original proposals, we argued that teachers in these schools should have an active voice in developing the teaching methods to be used and should also participate in such other decisions as the purchasing of materials. I don't think this is yet the case in most of the More Effective Schools. There again, it should be the function of the U.F.T. to stimulate its members to become more active in all facets of school life.

"It would be fine," Shapiro smiled, "if principals didn't require union impetus in this direction and would voluntarily, spontaneously, ask their teachers to assist in developing their schools' teaching plans and procedures."

Dr. Shapiro is also working on a long-range program, he explained, to increase the organized strength of atypical principals like himself. About four years ago he was one of the founders of the Union of School Supervisors. The older Council of Supervisory Associations comprises the overwhelming majority of the three thousand supervisory personnel in the system—principals, assistant principals, chairmen of departments, and supervisors of all kinds. By contrast, the Union of School Supervisors has only about one hundred members. "The Council," Shapiro said, "is asking for recognition as a collective bargaining unit but considers itself a professional group. We, however, regard ourselves as a labor union. We want to affiliate with the labor movement, because we feel that if an educator separates himself as a 'professional' from the great majority of working people, he is also separating himself from their aspirations and frustrations."

Despite the distinctly minority status of the Union of School Supervisors at present, Shapiro is sanguine about its potential for growth. "We came into being at a time when relatively few members of the U.F.T. had moved into supervisory positions. But, with more than thirty thousand of the forty thousand teachers in the system now in the union, we expect to be quite sizable in six to ten years, as more and more of those teachers become supervisory personnel. One of our goals will be to encourage teachers to become more creative in their teaching methods and to take much stronger roles in expanding democratic processes in the community as well as in the schools. The Council of Supervisory Associations, on the other hand, has yet to come out with any statement of its educational philosophy. Except," Shapiro smiled again, "for its opposition to ending the middle-class-biased group intelligence tests."

There was a parent waiting to see the principal. On the way out of his office, I asked about John. "He's still here," said Shapiro. "That is, he's on the register of a junior high school as attending a special progress class at P.S. 119, and next year he'll go into the eighth grade. His improvement has been such that he spends most of his time in class. He's in Mr. Knox's sixth-grade room." I remembered Mr. Knox as a tall, athletic-looking Negro, with considerable patience and sensitivity.

"There are still problems," Shapiro continued. "It's a relatively slow sixth-grade class, and John is very bright. When Knox is concentrating on the class as a whole, John will sometimes go on a sit-down strike. He won't cooperate. There are times when John unconsciously feels he needs someone near him when he does his work, and it's then that he resents Mr. Knox not giving his attention solely to him. But we're trying to get John to *see* that's what's going on and hopefully to grow out of it. There's not that much time left. He does have to go on to junior high school. Interestingly, though he still works in the office a little, John has been drawing away from me and identifying more and more with Mr. Knox. That's good."

XIII

In the corridor I saw Mrs. Lanckton, back again as a volunteer teacher. I asked her what she was specializing in during this school year. "It's supposed to be reading," she said, "but mostly it's just loving. Many of the children feel they're not at all important, that they won't amount to anything. It's no wonder some of them lose interest in reading. For a time, then, to get them to care about reading, they really need someone to read *to* them, to enjoy the pictures with them, to talk with them about a lot of things. About New York and home and loving and mothers and fathers. It's self-confidence they need; then the ABC's will come easier."

Mrs. Lanckton, I also discovered, had raised enough money to send John to camp for nine weeks in the summer that had just past. "He enjoyed it a great deal," she said. "Of course, he didn't tell me that right away. My first day back, he was so glad to see me he pretended he didn't know who I was. When I came into a room, he stormed out of it. But we're talking again. And there is marked improvement. Do you know the worst thing that's happened to him in school so far? When he had a fight with some kids in the yard, he was deprived for a time of the right to stay in his regular classroom. He could only just wander around the corridors. My, he was upset. But a year ago, who would have thought John would have so wanted to stay in a classroom?"

I dropped into see Miss Carmen Jones. The assistant principal was in her office, looking glumly at a sheaf of achievement scores. "I'm always dismayed," she said, "that some of our children do so poorly on tests. I go into classes and see children who are so bright and knowledgeable, who express themselves so freely. But often none of those qualities are reflected in their test scores. I don't know why. If I did, I'd do something about it. Sure, the scores show that we're doing a little better, but the scores are not good enough for the time and effort we put in. Part of it, I'm convinced, is that, even though we no longer have the group intelligence tests, there's a middle-class bias in the language used for the achievement tests. Much of the terminology is simply outside our children's experience. Look." She showed me a page of questions in a third-grade vocabulary test. "Trout. These kids don't know about trout. Their mothers buy porgies. And their fathers certainly don't go fishing. Well, we're going to have to give the children more practice in the types of tests they have to take."

I asked her view of teachers like Mr. Greenfield who feel that the child first has to feel important before he can learn. "Of course," she said, "I agree that the child must develop a strong ego. But I'm one of those old-fashioned people who believe the child needs the fundamentals in addition to a strong ego. We have to work on both. I'm old-fashioned about

John too. I have a hard time with him because my background leads me to expect children to defer to adults, to those in authority. But, on the other hand, if you believe the salvation of one child is worth any sacrifice, then perhaps the way Dr. Shapiro has treated John is justified. Who knows what John will become?"

Miss Jones was looking again at the test scores. "Some days," she said to me wearily, "I feel I'd get greater satisfaction if I were out digging ditches. At least at the end of the day, you can see you've made a hole."

The conversation with Miss Jones reminded me of a talk I'd had during the summer with a woman who has long been active in organizations committed to greater integration in the New York City public school system and to radical improvement in the education of all slum children. She has been a frequent visitor to P.S. 119 and is an admirer of Dr. Shapiro. "But there's still something wrong there," she had told me. "Those kids are not scoring as high as they should in the tests. It may be that all the understanding they get in that school, while it does help them develop a better self-image, doesn't help them to achieve. Shapiro and his teachers are certainly compassionate, but the children's parents are *ambitious* for their kids. Shapiro is like from another world. He has the kind of values all of us ought to have. But when they leave the school, those kids aren't going into his kind of world. They're going into a world that's increasingly competitive, and increasingly cybernated as well. Maybe it damages a kid to push him, but I keep wondering whether Shapiro isn't damaging them in another way. Are his kids going to have enough competitive drive to do more than survive?"

Later in the day, while we were walking again to the parking meter, I told Shapiro what the woman had said. "I agree with her," he began, "at least on the point that our children do not achieve enough. We're far behind. But as for the style of our school, just because they are going to have to be in a cybernated world, it's imperative that children remain human beings. In that respect, it's vital, for example, for children of all kinds of backgrounds to be in small enough classes so that they can have close and pleasurable relationships with adults. All of us are becoming more and more like I.B.M. machines in an increasingly organized and rationalized society, and all children ought to have the experience of real human contact, so they'll remember later on that human contact is both possible and pleasurable. And our children, of course, need that most of all.

"Getting back to achievement, you have to remember that our children are among the poorest of the poor. But they are achieving more, as a group, than children used to achieve here in the past. And again, part of the measure of their achievement is lost, because in the fourth grade we send out our best achievers to I.G.C. classes. The children, moreover, are also achieving the courage of their convictions. The very fact that Mr. Marcus' fifth-graders were able to write critically to publishers and to superintendents about the inadequacies of social studies textbooks is an indication they may have the spirit to contend with what lies ahead. It's most important to nurture that kind of spirit. Our children are Negro, and as young Negro adults, they'll have more than their proper share of responsibility for making the human race live like human beings."

Shapiro was silent for a minute or two. "However, there is disturbing validity in the criticism about underachievement, and it pertains to every school that is seriously understaffed." I asked Shapiro about an observation by one of the parents that at P.S. 119, it was the middle group—rather than the best and the worst of achievers—which was often overlooked. He nodded. "Around 1955," he said, "I became aware of the fact that no child in the school at the time was going to make it to college. It seemed to me that we therefore had to put a sizable amount of the resources we had into working with those children who seemed to be the most likely achievers. And since those resources were so slight, we had very little left over. Now, barring not too catastrophic circumstances in junior high school, in high school, in their lives, and in the community, twenty per cent of our children have a good chance to reach college. That's a great improvement, but the degree of our deprivation can be measured by the fact that sixty per cent of *all* children in the country are now reaching college.

"What of the others here? While we were focusing a great deal of energy and resources on the better achievers, we were also trying to make the entire school a place more favorable for, as it were, human contact—a freer place in which to teach and in which to be a child. Gradually, we were able thereby to develop a relatively stable staff, so that the middle range of children also would have a sequence of teachers who were relatively more experienced than those the children used to have here. And there has been some degree of improvement in the achievement of the middle children. But the fact remains that, after we get past the best achievers, there is a precipitous drop. We have a very long way to go. And we need a great deal of help."

We had stopped in front of the new school. Three stories high, its clean reddish-brown bricks and extensive window space made it look particularly cheerful by contrast with the gloomy battlements of P.S. 119. "Percival Goodman was the architect," Shapiro said. "He wouldn't take the job unless he was assured that the parents, teachers, and the principal would be involved in the planning. And we were. He and I also explored a relatively new school building in the next block. We walked all over it, including the roof. Its custodian was both astonished and pleased to see us. It was the first time in his experience that anyone had examined the drawbacks of one new building before going ahead to build another.

"We didn't get everything we wanted from headquarters at Livingston Street. Almost all the new elementary schools have a capacity of twelve hundred children—forty classrooms with thirty kids in each. We asked for seventy classrooms with twenty children in each. The compromise was fifty-five classrooms. Theoretically, fourteen hundred children are to be distributed among them, but I won't permit the number to go above eleven hundred.

"Goodman worked a long time on the designs, and in some ways, the school is really well planned. For example, very few, if any, of the new schools have an inside play area that can be used during inclement weather. The children have to stand in the halls or sit in the auditoriums or lunchrooms. Putting that much constraint on children during what should be their free periods leads to a lot of hostility when they go back to the classroom. But we have an inside play area. Also, there's a great deal more soundproofing in this school than has been put into any other so far, and as a result, we can encourage livelier activities without too much concern that the noise will bother neighboring classrooms. And a special unit for disturbed children has been set up—two classrooms with an office. Those have been especially soundproofed. But we may have to give that unit up. If P.S. 92 does become a More Effective School, we'll have small enough classes so that we won't need a particular unit for children with problems. Another asset is a somewhat larger library than any other elementary school has had up to this point. It's still not as big as I'd like, but that was another compromise."

A few days later, I found Shapiro involved in studying and advising a new project in teacher-training for slum schools. Early in 1965, the Coordinating Council on Education for the Disadvantaged had been formed as a clearinghouse for information on education of children who have been discriminated against. It also helps develop new programs and tries to act as a liaison between various elements in the community committed to basic improvements in this area of education. Its support comes primarily from the labor movement and civil rights groups; and its chairman is Benjamin F. McLaurin, an official of the Brotherhood of Sleeping Car Porters and a member of the New York City Board of Higher Education.

The Council had now devised a plan to train sizable numbers of new teachers, particularly members of minority groups and particularly men, as specialists in the education of poverty-stricken children. The recruits, largely consisting of liberal arts graduates with the desire but not the financial resources to become teachers, would be interns assigned to schools requiring special services. Since the interns would be paid from Federal and possibly foundation funds, those schools could have smaller adult-to-pupil ratios without additional cost to the city. Under the supervision of a regular teacher, the interns would work with small groups of children in both remedial instruction and on new material. Corollary institutes, seminars, and workshops, staffed by faculty members from cooperating colleges, would also be provided the interns after school hours. In a year or a little more, the interns would be able to earn a master's degree and then enter the school system as regular teachers.

The initial goal was to be two hundred and sixty-five interns to be recruited by minority-group teachers in the school system, civil rights groups, colleges, and other organizations.

"The possibilities are very exciting," Shapiro said as he gave me the news. "Just informally, I asked thirty-five Negro teachers about potential recruits, and each knew at least

one person who would like to become a teacher if there were
financial backing for his training. You know, for example,
there are any number of Negro men who were graduated
from college in the early 1950s—some from law schools as
well—who are working as mail clerks and in similar jobs.
We can raise enough funds so that if the project goes through,
we'll simultaneously be giving more children the experience
of a small world in which adults protect them and we'll be
bringing teachers into the system who can more easily
identify with the children. Not only teachers. Some of the
interns might be trained as guidance counselors and as
catalysts to get people in poor neighborhoods to organize
themselves for social action.

"The training will be in the direction of developing an
organic relationship between the interns and the life of the
school and the community—much more so than in any other
proposed teacher-internship program I know about. That's
why I'm happy the United Federation of Teachers is involved
in this. The interns and the cooperating teachers need to feel
free to criticize, to experiment, to become part of the life of
the community without fear of retaliation.

"We've also received evidences of support from the United
Parents' Associations. the Board of Education, and the Board
of Higher Education, the latter being in charge of the city
universities and colleges from which we'll get our specialists.
The interns will be encouraged to participate in parents'
association meetings, and they'll sit in on conferences with
neighborhood people, welfare investigators, church leaders,
and other elements in the community. They'll get to be able
to analyze housing problems, for instance, and once they
know what can be done, they'll also know the degree to
which they can most effectively participate—and in what
ways. I've already drawn up a list of possible courses for
the interns."

Shapiro handed me a paper. At the top of his list was the notation: "Most, if not all, of the courses should be of a workshop or practicum type, immediately related to the classroom experiences of the interns." Among the suggested courses were:

The relationship of different educational philosophies to classroom management, activities and experiences.

Methods and principles of teaching as developed from the classroom experiences of the interns.

Methods and principles of teaching reading and mathematics through analyzing the classroom experiences of interns.

Methods and principles for presenting the history of Africa and the contributions of the American Negro to American History.

Analysis of the deficiencies of social studies textbooks in order to develop a desirable social studies curriculum.

Dynamics of a changing society as observed in classroom activities and experiences.

The psychology of expressive behavior of children and teachers as observed in the classroom experiences of the interns.

The psychology of normal and of abnormal behavior of children and teachers as observed in the class.

The psychology of the motivation of human behavior.

The psychology of individual differences.

Seminar in educational research.

Methods and materials for studying Latin-American cultures.

Spanish for teachers from Puerto Rico.

Critique of research in language arts, curriculum, and teaching.

Principles and methods of developing original, creative

dramatizations that would reflect the problems of the community.

The role in the school life of teachers' organizations and participation in them.

"I don't know when this project will be able to start," said Shapiro as he took back the paper. "There are obstacles. There is always resistance to change in education, especially when the ideas for change come from outside what might be considered the establishments. There's not just one; there are several educational establishments. And they prefer concepts they've thought up themselves.

"In the meantime," Shapiro stood up, "there are the immediate problems. This fall we set up one third-grade class of only nineteen. We selected children who seemed to have the greatest disparity between their ability and their achievement so far in reading. It has been indicated to me from above that we can't afford the luxury of a class with an adult-to-pupil ratio of one-to-nineteen. Well, I've remained adamant on the subject."

I followed him into the corridor. Shapiro paused at a window and looked out at a group of older boys playing basketball in the yard. They seemed to be fifteen or sixteen, and they appeared to be playing hooky from wherever they were supposed to be.

I asked Shapiro about the growing belief among some educators involved in preschool training for slum children that, if a child is not sufficiently stimulated to learn in elementary school, irreparable damage has been done in terms of his capacity to achieve later. "No," he said. "I don't believe it. It does make a real difference if you catch them earlier, and it's easier to reach them early. Also, there probably is a net loss if the child is caught quite late. And if the attempt isn't made until late, much more resources are needed. But I don't believe they're beyond help. Look at those boys. I know them. They can hardly read, but they certainly do have hostility; and if they could become involved, let us say, in action against slum landlords and in similar projects to change the community, they'd be motivated to learn to read in order to be more effective in what they were trying to do."

As we walked to the gym, I asked Shapiro if there was still doubt that P.S. 119 would be torn down, as promised, to provide a play area for the new school. "I'm now convinced it will be," he said. "But what," I asked "of the considerable investment in repairs that was suddenly put into P.S. 119?" He grinned. "That is simply another illustration of the surrealism of the school system."

Inside the gym, amid the roar and rush of children, a small boy, crying, came up to Shapiro. The principal leaned over, listened intently, and said, "I'll get the ball back for you. You stay here." He moved swiftly across the floor, talked to two sixth-graders playing basketball, and came back to the boy. "They'll be finished soon. You stay here."

Two girls from a kindergarten class came up to Shapiro. The principal leaned over again, listened, and as one of the girls took his hand, he moved quickly into the lunchroom. "Do you maybe have two oranges?" he asked an aide. She did, and he gave each girl an orange. They skipped away. "Their teacher," Shapiro explained, peering around the gym, "had promised everyone an orange, but those two had forgotten their coats. When they came back, the teacher was gone. Now where's that boy?" Shapiro couldn't find the little boy who had first stopped him when he'd come into the gym. The principal looked disturbed. "That was a retarded child. Two bigger kids had taken away his ball, and I told him I'd get it back as soon as they finished a few points. I didn't want them to

be so angry they'd beat him up later. But I made a mistake.
I should have stayed until they were through. The girls
would have waited. Well, the boy's gone. Now he thinks I
betrayed him."

A neatly dressed boy of about nine, holding a small brief-
case, rushed up to Shapiro. He was crying loudly. Shapiro
hugged him and took him over to a teacher. "He couldn't
find his older sister," Shapiro said to me. "She takes him
home. He was crying because he was afraid he wouldn't
know how to get home. He's been here three years, and he
lives near by. Is he retarded? Or is it some other problem? It's
hard to tell."

A boy whizzed over to Shapiro, whispered to him excitedly,
and whizzed away. "He saw a boy break a window near the
door. It was apparently done quite deliberately. This one says
he'll point out the boy who did it when they line up in the
morning. I took him seriously, not because I want to encourage snitching, but because he feels so strongly that it
was wrong to break the window, and I have to go along
with him. If he remembers to come over to me tomorrow
morning, I'll have to follow through."

On the far side of the gym, John was shooting at a basket.
He saw Shapiro and waved. The principal waved back. "He's
having a good day," said Shapiro. "There's another complica-
tion this year. The older youngsters on the block where John
lives have been caught up in black nationalism. He hangs
out with them, but at school he's with an integrated group of
people he's come to trust somewhat. So there's a conflict. And
when he gets particularly frustrated here, the racial epithets
come flying out. But the epithets are bi-racial. He'll call me
a white something or other, and he'll call a teacher a black
something or other. It's hard for him."

A very little child, perhaps five, was alone in the center of
the floor. He was crying. Shapiro went over, picked him up,

touched his head to his, listened through the sobs, and brought him to a teacher. "He'd lost his class," said Shapiro when he came back.

We left the gym, and as we came toward his office, I remembered the conversation I'd had the previous spring with several teachers fantasizing Shapiro in the role of Superintendent of Schools. "What *would* you do?" I asked. He obviously enjoyed the chance to speculate.

"I'd go to all the poorest neighborhoods and stir up the parents. I'd have a few offices—not just one—and most would be in the poor communities. I'd travel to them on a regular schedule, so that the parents would know when I'd be there if they wanted to see me. My main office would be in Harlem or in Bedford-Stuyvesant. I'd also approach as many groups throughout the city as possible to get as much community support for the funds we need. The middle class. The business community. I'd make it very clear to them they haven't been helping nearly enough. And I'd constantly urge the Board of Education to demand larger budgets. Constantly.

"Also," Shapiro continued, "I'd set up a permanent office in Washington, because much of the funding from now on has to be Federally based. In that office we'd develop specialists in formulating programs and in knowing how to get them through all the various agencies in that governmental maze. Then we'd have to relate their specialized knowledge to the political strength of New York City. In other words, we'd have to devise ways to keep the populace alert as to who has been helping education, and hopefully their votes would signify their continuing concern. That's the beginning."

"It would certainly be a lively administration," I said.

"To say the least," Shapiro smiled. The bench in the outer office was nearly full of waiting children.

Epilogue

The exodus from P.S. 119 to the new three-story P.S. 92 (the Mary McLeod Bethune School) took place on February 26, 1966.

For days before, the children had been impatient in their anticipation. At the drugstore on 135th Street and Eighth Avenue, where many of the children congregate, a counterman told of a third-grader who talked of little else but the move to the new school. "I even see me in that school in my dreams," the small boy said.

On the afternoon before the move, in the yard of P.S. 119, Elliott Shapiro announced that this would be everyone's last day at the old school, which was going to be torn down and turned into a playground for P.S. 92.

An explosion of cheering was triggered by his announcement. "I was kind of surprised," Shapiro said later, "by such a unanimous expression of strong feeling. Sometimes, after all, you think nostalgically about an old school. But the cheering signified we were all worn out by this building. When we lined up the next morning," he continued, "the children were all in high spirits. There was an irresistible eagerness to get going and a lack of desire to look back. I felt the same way. To be sure, I had spent twelve years in that building, and you might have thought I'd have a touch of regret at leaving it. But like the children and the staff, I was glad to put it—even to push it—into the past."

At 10:15 in the morning, the children's march began—up West 133rd Street, across Eighth Avenue, and along West 134th Street. A band from a local junior high school played, the children sang, and finally they were settled in the new school, which had been brought into being by the concerted, combined insistence of the children's parents, their teachers, and their principal.

John was not in the march. The previous November, Shapiro, several members of his staff, and the Bureau of Attendance caseworker who had been seeing John regularly decided not to hold him in the elementary school for another year. One reason was that at P.S. 119, the presence of younger children was a constant source of temptation to John to test how far he could go, how aggressive he could be. "We had been as supportive of John as we could," Shapiro pointed out, "while still protecting the younger children. But by this point, a kind of sibling rivalry had been built up so that by being strong enough with him in terms of the younger children, we would also appear to him to be rejecting him. And so we felt he ought to be in a school where he couldn't pick on younger children.

"Also," Shapiro continued, "he was testing us by his actions in Mr. Knox's class. It was not an advanced sixth-grade class and he was supposed to be doing seventh-grade work in it. John resented that his work was harder than that of the others in the class, and he'd make an issue of it in such a way that it couldn't be contained in the classroom and flowed out into the halls and through the rest of the building.

"It seemed to us, after talking it over carefully, that it was necessary to indicate to John that you can't go through the foundation of reality and survive. We had to show him reality did have a foundation. And when we told him we had decided to transfer him to another school, he appeared to take the decision with a feeling of relief. He saw that there was a borderline of behavior—a limit—beyond which he could not go. You see, if he felt that there were no limits, the world—in his unconscious—would seem to be too dangerous to cope with."

First John was sent to a junior high school in the area. "We were concerned," says Shapiro, "because we knew he'd have to deal with six to eight different teachers and might get into trouble the very first day."

John did get into trouble on the very first day, but in a way that underlined his considerable potential for more than survival. From neighborhood children, he had learned the names of the most punitive teachers in the school; and on that first day, when John saw that he had been assigned to the classes of several of those teachers, he absolutely refused to attend the school. He created such a furor that he was almost suspended then and there.

Through the Bureau of Attendance caseworker, it was possible to send John instead to a disguised 600 School where the classes are smaller. He is having some difficulties there, still testing the pressures of the outside world, but at the same time adapting to some routines and responsibilities about which he used to make an explosive issue.

On Fridays, John returns to the elementary school, and Shapiro gives him two dollars "so that he can have a good weekend." John never says he misses the principal, but, Shapiro adds, "every once in a while, he makes a tender gesture—reaching out a hand to touch my shoulder."

Shapiro himself is still involved with strategy to get the new school into the More Effective Schools program. And there are teachers to hire for the next year. "In the fall," he says with anticipation, "we're getting some civil rights people on the staff. For a new teacher one of my basic criteria is that he or she has been involved in the civil rights movement or in the Peace Corps."

A major disappointment to Shapiro has been the defeat of the Coordinating Council on Education's project for teacher-training in the slum schools that would have focused on male members of minority groups as teaching interns within an unusually democratic context of training, teaching, and participation in the needs of the neighborhood. "We appear to have lost that fight, for the time being," said Shapiro, "because it was too great a threat to the various educational establishments and bureaucracies. And thereby we lose an opportunity to do something basic to democratize everybody involved in education."

Meanwhile, at P.S. 92, daily there are the children with complaints to answer, with hurts that require comforting, with achievements to encourage. Persistently, there is also the question of group achievement. In some elementary schools in the city, there is great and growing emphasis on practicing for the city-wide achievement tests, but Shapiro wonders what that implies and whether it is an aid to the children or rather to the school system's image of itself.

"Here," he says, "we tend to frown on that degree of emphasis on practicing, and so when the scores come out, we're penalized a bit. But we do have the advantage of knowing what we actually are achieving and what we're not achieving. When it's suggested that we practice more, I ask aloud whether the scores would then have any meaning. You know what I'm told? 'Use a code!'

"This pressure to practice has become very strong. When a very high echelon superintendent sets the reading-score minimum requirement for promotion six months or so *above the district average,* he is either ignorant or he is telling us to get much higher scores in any old way. Aside from the dishonesty, or ignorance, inherent in this, the children, by practicing for the specific tests, may get higher reading scores but will actually be reading just as poorly. And thereby the need for additional resources and for smaller classes will be concealed by the false scores. By putting that much emphasis on scores without substance, things will become worse than ever for our children. But at this school I'm resisting that route.

"On the day we moved, Mayor John Lindsay came, and there was considerable coverage by the press and by television. I, our teachers, and parent after parent emphasized during the interviews the urgent need for including P.S. 92 in the More Effective Schools program. If, we kept saying, as a More Effective School, we had more teachers and other additional professional assistants, we could make tremendous progress. As of now, three-quarters to four-fifths of our children are being virtually disqualified from real participation in the society. But in a More Effective School, perhaps four-fifths of them would get the foundation to be able to participate in American life, such as it is.

"Except for one television station," Shapiro concluded, "neither the newspaper nor other reporters there picked up the essence of what we were saying. So we have to go on fighting so that more of our children do not die."

In March 1966, at a turbulent hearing before the New York

City Board of Education, a mother from East Harlem pierced
through the din and told Board President Lloyd K. Garrison,
"What you see is sheer frustration. Despite all your glorious
pronouncements about reorganization, the children are still
being crippled. We don't want to lose another generation of
children."

The Board, meanwhile, had made no move to extend
the More Effective Schools program. And then on April 15,
1966, the Mayor announced that although the Board had
asked for $76.5 million for improvements, in the 1966–67
budget it would be given only $18.7 million for that purpose.

In the City of New York, as in cities throughout the
United States, public education, particularly in the ghettos, is
still financed on a principle of scarcity.

At P.S. 92, the thrust for life continues. And P.S. 119 is
being torn down. How many children since 1899 have already
been buried there?

As for John, the odds are still against him. But how much
higher would they have been had Elliott Shapiro not been
his principal? After reading John's story, Paul A. Fine, who
prepared *Neighbors of the President: A Study of the Patterns
of Youth Life in the Second Precinct, Washington, D.C.* for
the President's Committee on Juvenile Delinquency and
Youth Crime, wrote to Shapiro:

> To see that someone like John is a "normal" child whose "ab-
> normal" reactions are perfectly "normal"—given the situations to
> which he must react—is to have a faith in people that few of
> us possess. And it means taking risks. We are, despite the
> mythology, not a risk-taking society. We move with power
> to clobber those we fear. We demand guarantees before we
> buy. We do not take risks. *We* are the neurotics, and these are
> our defense mechanisms.
>
> We do not have the "inner discipline" nor the confidence to
> allow people like John to test himself against us and to dis-

cover his strength through ours. Yet the only true hope for ourselves and for John lies in this faith, born of trust, carried with the courage and strength that can take necessary risks. Any other approach is a guarantee—of safety perhaps, but of defeat of human purpose certainly.

And is it a guarantee even of safety?